BBC

DOCTOR WHO

BORROWED TIME

BORROWED TIME

1 3 5 7 9 10 8 6 4 2

BBC Books, an imprint of Ebury Publishing.
20 Vauxhall Bridge Road,
London SW1V 2SA

BBC Books is part of the Penguin Random House group of companies,
whose addresses can be found at global.penguinrandomhouse.com

Doctor Who is a BBC Wales production for BBC One.
Executive Producers: Steven Moffat, Piers Wenger and Beth Willis

First published by BBC Books in 2011
This edition published in 2018

www.penguin.co.uk

A CIP catalogue record for this book is available from the British Library.

ISBN 978 1 785 94372 0

Publishing Director: Albert DePetrillo
Cover design by David Wardle © Woodlands Books Ltd, 2018
Production: Phil Spencer

Printed and bound in Great Britain by Clays Ltd, St Ives PLC

Penguin Random House is committed to a sustainable future for our business,
our readers and our planet. This book is made from Forest Stewardship
Council® certified paper.

This book is for my brother, Eliot Alderman.
Because Doctor Who *has always been the place we share.*
And for my cousin Samuel West, whose request that I should write something for him to read was where this book began.

'Compound interest is the most powerful force in the universe.'
Albert Einstein (allegedly)

'Only in mathematics will we find truth.'
Cardinal Borusa

The view on the monitors was dark. Occasionally, a line of numbers scrolled past, faster than any human eye could have followed them. But mostly, it was dark. It was dark, in a sense, all the time. But then, 'all the time' is a relative concept. A lot can happen in a slice of time too infinitesimally small to be measured on any human scale. So, occasionally there was a burst of frenetic activity. But mainly, it was dark.

The monitors were mounted on the walls of the large, high room, facing in towards a central well, which was empty. Well, mostly it was empty. Occasionally, for an infinitely tiny period of time, it was more full than would have been possible if some very advanced trans-dimensional physics weren't being used.

If you'd stood in the middle of that empty central well for an hour, you would have been fine, on the whole. Bored, even. You would have stood there staring at the dark monitors, letting your eyes adjust to the gloom. You would have looked up at the huge glass domes still radiating a tiny amount of light, just enough to see by, and the enormous tall arched windows with their thousands of individual panes, and the curved marble walls and ceiling vaulting high above you and you'd have been impressed by the grandeur of the building but nothing more. You'd have tried to see out of the windows which are too tall for anyone of human stature to see anything from but the stars and the moons. You might have looked at those three blood-red moons for a while, appreciatively or apprehensively, depending on your temperament.

But in that hour, there would have been a single sliver of time. Let's round it up and say that it would have been one-hundredth of a second. In that sliver of time it would have seemed to you that all your senses were being hammered on at once. That, suddenly, the lights were too bright and too strangely coloured and the place was full of steaming, smelly bodies and there were angry shouting voices in a thousand languages you couldn't understand, and the monitors were alive with flickering numbers and letters and an image of a man in a tweed jacket bound hand and foot, and the thing would have been so overwhelmingly terrifying that you would have screamed out.

And found you were screaming in an empty, dark hall. You would have whirled around, sure that something terrible had just been done to you. Your heart would have been pounding, your pupils dilated, your skin prickling with terror. But the hall would still have been quiet, and empty, with only the thin grey light from the globes high above you and the blood-red moons outside the windows. There would have been nothing else to see, or touch, and no way to understand what had just happened to you.

Unless, of course, you'd been able to slow down time. And then you would have seen something else entirely.

Chapter 1

Mr Symington and Mr Blenkinsop entered Andrew Brown's life on possibly the worst morning of his career.

It hadn't been, up to that point, a particularly stellar career. Andrew Brown wasn't a high-flier, more of a low-glider. He wasn't a big shot, more of a small fry. He'd got a good degree from a good university and hadn't known quite what to do with himself after he left. The man at the careers service had dipped a digestive biscuit into his tea and pulled a flyer apparently at random from a pile next to him.

'Lexington International Bank are holding a recruitment day next week,' the careers adviser had said, failing to bite into his biscuit before it disintegrated, and then failing to catch it before it collapsed soggily onto the floor. 'Oh damn,' he said, trying to wipe up the mess.

'But I…' Andrew had said.

The careers adviser tried to scrape the biscuit up with some papers before apparently noticing that they were important and trying to scrape the biscuit off them instead. It seemed to Andrew that he'd half-forgotten him already as he said:

'Try Lexington, blue chip company, good place to work, worth a go.'

Andrew Brown wondered sometimes if his life would have been totally different if the biscuit had been a bourbon instead. They take longer to dissolve in tea.

He tested well, that was the thing. Put him in front of a problem and he'd try to solve it. Put him in front of an exam and he'd try to ace it. Put him in front of a ladder and he'd try to climb it – without necessarily looking at what that ladder was leaning against or working out whether he really wanted to be up at the top of it. He'd sat down in front of the Lexington International Bank aptitude test and tried hard to solve every question. He'd worked hard at the corporate recruitment away-days on building a raft out of tyres and troubleshooting an imaginary failing business. He got on well with most people. He was an excellent team player – this had been noted on the letter Lexington Bank had sent him offering him a job.

That had been ten years ago, though, and he was still climbing that ladder. After starting as a graduate trainee, he now worked at Lexington International Bank as a financial analyst. Mostly, this meant that he read about companies, put some numbers about them into spreadsheets, and made random guesses about whether they'd make more or less money over the next six months. He sat in front of a computer for twelve hours a day trying to impress the people higher up than him so that they'd advance him one more rung on that imaginary ladder and give him the money that he'd convinced himself made it all almost worthwhile. The thing about the Lexington International Bank ladder was that it was very long, and climbing it was very exhausting, and so Andrew Brown didn't have a lot of time to think about whether he really wanted to get to the top of it – and besides, since so many other people were climbing too, the view from the top must be worth it.

So he kept going. He worked hard. He put his heart and mind and soul into it. There was an opening for a position half a rung higher than he already was. With a promotion, he might get two hours a week of a secretary's time. He'd go to more important meetings, with more senior people, and have the opportunity to impress them, and if he did he might be promoted again and then... well, of course eventually he'd be running the whole office. It's important to have a dream: otherwise you might notice where you really are.

Today's meeting was particularly important. The new head of the London office, Vanessa Laing-Randall, would be there. She was notoriously hard to please, but if he impressed her then his career would take off. Only one serious rival stood between him and that promotion: the always aggravatingly well-prepared Sameera Jenkins. She'd been snapping at his heels all year, she always had just one more fact at her disposal, had worked just one extra hour on a project. But he had her this time, he knew it. No one could have been better prepared than Andrew Brown. That promotion was his: he could taste it.

He woke up on the morning of the important meeting feeling well rested and calm. He could hear birdsong through his window, the quiet sounds of the suburban street outside and… wait a minute. Well rested? Calm? A sudden horrifying terror gripped him.

He sat up and, almost unable to bear it, forced himself to look at the 5 a.m. alarm he'd set on his mobile phone. The phone's face was blank. Dead. Had it broken? He looked again, a terrible hollow feeling opening up in his stomach. He'd forgotten to plug the charger in. It had run out of battery. Heart pounding, breathing hard, he leapt out of bed and dashed out to look at the clock in the hall. It was 6.45 a.m. Andrew Brown swore loudly, and at length.

But it was OK, it was all right. He'd intended to get into the office very early, by 5.45 a.m. to give his presentation another run-through, to check his photocopies were all in order. He could leave now, eat his toast on the way to the station, and be at the office with half an hour to spare before the 8.30 a.m. meeting. It'd be fine.

He dashed back into his bedroom, stubbing his toe hard on the bedside table but that didn't matter, no time to deal with that blinding pain now, and oh god was his toe bleeding? Should he put a plaster on it? No time, put on socks, pants, shave quickly, but not too quickly wouldn't want to turn up with a lacerated face. Right, OK, shaved, now put on the suit he'd laid out specially the night before and… what the hell was that?

He blinked at his suit, laid out efficiently on a chair by his bedside table which now had a spreading water patch over the trousers. It took him a full thirty-eight seconds to realise that when he'd stubbed his toe on the bedside table he'd also knocked over his glass of water, which had fallen on his trousers.

Could he wear another suit? But this was his best one, the one his sister Sara said made him look both dashing and professional. Iron, then. Where did he even keep the iron? He looked in four different cupboards and found it. He switched it on. He touched it to see if it was hot. He burned his hand. He ironed his trousers until the wet patch disappeared. His phone rang. Had the meeting started early? Were they calling to find out where he was? He answered it as he tried, one-handed, to hop into his trousers.

'Andrew, it's Sara. I know it's early but I knew you'd be awake.'

'Hi, sis, I'm…' He had half a piece of toast in his mouth. He had one leg in his trousers, and was gripping the phone between his ear and his shoulder.

'Yeah, I know, Andrew, I know, you're really busy, you're running late…'

As he tried to manoeuvre his foot into the trousers, he lost his balance, collided with the ironing board, the iron fell off onto the carpet and the phone bounced onto the floor. He managed to pull his trousers up, pick up the iron, sustaining another small burn to his hand, do up his belt and then put the phone back to his ear in time to hear his sister say:

'So do you have anything to say to me, Andrew?'

'I, um…'

'I'm waiting.'

'I really am very late, actually. I really have to… I'm really sorry, I have to go.'

'So you don't want to wish me Happy Birthday or anything?'

'I….' Andrew looked at the place on the carpet where

the hot iron had made a dark burn. He sighed. He should have remembered. He'd meant to send flowers. And a card. He'd meant to buy a present.

'I'm sorry, sis, I'm really sorry. Happy Birthday. I'll make it up to you, OK?'

'Yeah, yeah, sure. And I'll tell your niece and nephew you'll definitely see them before they're 40, OK?'

He looked at his watch. It was 7.03 a.m. There was a train at 7.11 a.m. that would get him into the office a full twenty minutes before the meeting was due to start. The station was a ten-minute walk away. He ran. After five minutes, the station was in sight! There was a train at the platform! The train was early! He put on a burst of speed. But as he hurtled through the barrier, the train pulled away from the station. He checked the sign. That wasn't the 7.11 a.m. It was the delayed 6.48 a.m. The trains were running twenty minutes late.

He called his office from the payphone at the station, and tried to make things better. He left messages but no one picked up. They wouldn't postpone the meeting for him.

When he finally got onto a packed train, his heart was pounding ceaselessly. He gripped the rail he was clinging to as if he could make the train go faster just by mentally commanding it to.

From the station he ran all the way to the office. His best, ironed suit was sticky with sweat. He realised his shirt couldn't have dried properly when he last washed it, because the sweat was making it smell of mildew. He kept on running. When he saw that the lifts were jammed, he even ran up the stairs to the seventh floor. He arrived, sweating and panting, and smelly and with a stain on his crotch that he realised looked suspiciously like something wet had been there.

He was just in time to see Sameera Jenkins, flawless, elegant Sameera, come to the end of her presentation. To hear the round of applause from his boss, and his boss's boss and Vanessa Laing-Randall herself. It was all Andrew Brown could do not to burst into tears.

He did try to give his presentation. Even after they told him that really the meeting was over. There was no more time. He persuaded them to give him just five minutes to show what he'd done.

But he hadn't had enough time to try out his presentation on the computer in the conference room. The slides didn't work properly. Where he'd thought there'd be a chart of Fiscal Growth there was only a note saying 'Fiscal Growth chart goes here'. Where he'd hoped for a burst of rousing music to finish off his presentation, the computer used the wrong sound file and there was a long loud slow low note. It sounded like a fart. He felt tears starting in his eyes and thought nothing could possibly be worse than showing his emotions in front of all these senior people – not to mention Sameera Jenkins, smirking like a cat – so he thanked them, in a strained voice, for their time and walked back to his desk.

He sat at his desk and stared blankly at his rows of files, seeing nothing but the pitying faces of the people round that meeting room table.

And then, without his ever subsequently being able to remember how it had happened, Mr Symington and Mr Blenkinsop were in his office.

They were two middle-aged white men, dressed in neat, identical black wool suits and white shirts with a faint blue pinstripe. One of them wore a dark green tie, the other wore a dark blue tie. They had the kind of totally ordinary, clean-shaven, innocuous faces that you'd forget the moment they left the room. Andrew Brown hadn't heard them knock, or invited them in. But he forgot that as soon as they were there. They seemed like the kind of people you didn't have to invite in. They probably belonged everywhere.

'Good morning,' said the slightly shorter, thinner one with the dark green tie. 'I'm Mr Symington. This is my associate.'

'Good morning to you, Mr Andrew Brown,' said the slightly taller, stockier man with the dark blue tie, 'I'm Mr Blenkinsop.'

'Good, er, morning,' said Andrew Brown.

'Although, in fact, we hear you've had a bad morning, Mr Brown,' said Mr Symington.

'Yes indeed,' said Mr Blenkinsop. 'We're sorry to mention it, really, sorry to bring it up at all, but you know, Mr Brown, we all have a bad morning sometimes.'

'Couldn't have put it better myself, Mr Blenkinsop,' said Mr Symington. 'Bad mornings are a very common event. That's why the service we offer is so valuable.'

'Service?' Andrew couldn't help himself asking.

'We're glad you asked, Mr Brown, very glad indeed,' said Mr Symington. 'Aren't we, Mr Blenkinsop?'

'That we are, Mr Symington. Because you see, we represent a consortium, Mr Brown, that's right, a consortium of like-minded businesspeople, people with time, as you might say, on their hands. People who have more of it than they rightly know what to do with, isn't that right, Mr Symington?'

'Certainly is, Mr Blenkinsop, it certainly is. Yes, you see our colleagues – that is to say the consortium of highly leveraged businesspeople we represent – are able to make you an offer today which is beyond your wildest dreams. That's right. Quite literally, beyond the wildest dream you have ever dreamed, even after a dinner consisting only of Brie, Camembert and Wisconsin Sharp Cheddar.'

The two men laughed in perfect unison.

Mr Symington continued: 'How would you feel if you could get an extra hour any time you liked? That's right, an extra hour to play golf, to polish up that report for your boss, to spend time with your girlfriend or indeed boyfriend – we don't want to appear prejudiced, do we, Mr Blenkinsop? – or just to sleep late? Think what that could do for you – an extra hour! Can't you just imagine it, Mr Blenkinsop?'

'Why, yes I can, Mr Symington. Just think of it. Every businessman or businesswoman knows that, sometimes, an hour before breakfast is worth three hours in the afternoon. Take today, for example. Wouldn't you happily, eagerly, give up the rest of the day just to have had two extra hours this morning? Imagine if you could manage your time like that!' Mr Blenkinsop nudged him in the ribs sharply. 'There'd be no stopping you climbing up the career ladder then, would there, Mr Brown?'

Andrew blinked at the two men. There was something a little odd about their appearance – not their clothes, which were ordinary, conservative business suits – but their very being. They were fuzzy at the edges. When he tried to focus on their faces, they became blurred. It really was a most disturbing sensation.

'Look,' he said, 'I've got so much work to do, and the day's gone horribly wrong already. Do you have something to sell me? A book on time-management, is that it?'

Mr Symington and Mr Blenkinsop smiled at each other and turned back to Andrew.

'Better than that.'

'Far, far better than that.'

'Mr Brown, we can loan you time.'

'That's right, Mr Brown. We can lend you as much time as you need. As much time as you can handle. As much time as you could ever desire.'

'We can lend you enough time to get all your preparation done for this morning's meeting. The time to spend with friends and family. The time to get ahead of... what's her name, Mr Blenkinsop?'

'Sameera Jenkins, Mr Symington. Nasty little upstart. Unlike our friend Mr Brown.'

'Deserves what's coming to her, if you ask me. And Mr Brown will give it to her. He just needs a little help. Now of course, Mr Brown, that time will have to be paid back.'

'At what we think you'll agree,' muttered Mr Blenkinsop, just a little too fast for Andrew to fully catch, 'is a very reasonable rate of interest.'

'Imagine what it could do for your career. All the time you want, Mr Brown, at the touch of a button.'

They paused. The men turned to Andrew and looked at him, as if daring him to call them liars. And suddenly, Andrew Brown felt very angry. Here he was, on the worst day of his life, and these two jokers were playing him for a fool.

'Loan me... What on earth are you talking about? Look, how did you get in here? Who are you? You'd better show me some identification, or I'm going to call security!'

'He doesn't believe us, Mr Symington.'

'They so rarely do, Mr Blenkinsop.'

'I think a demonstration is in order, Mr Symington.'

'Certainly is, Mr Blenkinsop.'

And from his back pocket, Mr Symington produced his demonstration. And then everything became very clear indeed to Andrew Brown.

Chapter 2

The sunset, it seemed to Amy, had been going on for about five hundred years. She stared at it some more. Rory's arm was around her shoulders, they were snuggled up together on a picnic blanket. They were on a beach covered with white-gold sand. Tiny blue-green iridescent crabs scuttled at the water's edge. Fifty-first-century Earth had certainly cleaned up since her day – there was no litter anywhere in sight. Out at sea, a dolphin occasionally crested the surface of the ocean, leaping for the pure joy of being alive. The sunset was ochre and amber, a glorious warm light spreading across the sky and reflected ripplingly in the water. Even the scent of the place was gorgeous, all coconut and tropical flowers. It was, as far as she knew, literally the most romantic place in space and time. And she was bored.

'How long has this sunset been going on now?'

Rory flinched.

'The whole point is not to think about time, Amy. Just –' he breathed in deeply and breathed out slowly –

'relax. Drink it in.'

Amy wriggled her shoulders. Stopped staring at the sunset. Stopped watching the tiny crabs frolicking at her toes. Turned instead and stared at Rory.

'But seriously,' she said slowly. 'How. Long?'

She stared into his eyes, unblinking. It was a game they'd played since they were children. Seeing who could go longest without blinking. She always won.

Rory blinked. He hadn't even been trying.

He looked down at the Super Lucky Romance Camera: Capture the Moment!™ on the picnic blanket next to him.

'Um,' he said, 'I think it's been about three hours? This sunset? About three hours?'

'Three. Hours?!'

Amy stood up and stalked over to the edge of their Super Lucky Romance Bubble, the place where the air shimmered slightly. She kicked at it. The Super Lucky Romance Bubble wobbled, making the view of the infinitely prolonged sunset wobble too. The Bubble was about twenty metres wide and about forty metres tall at its highest point. A lovely large space to play in. If you weren't already very bored.

'And how much longer is it going on for?'

Rory consulted the Super Lucky Romance Camera.

'Doesn't say. It's… I think it's supposed to be a surprise?'

Amy let out a growl and flung herself onto her back on the picnic blanket. Rory stretched out a consoling hand.

'It's supposed to be romantic… You, me, a single moment of time prolonged for several hours so we can fully experience it here in our little bubble... and... didn't mind so much the other day when we...'

Rory's brain finally got the message to his mouth that he should Just Stop Talking. Amy looked at Rory's hand hovering just above her shoulder. He wondered if she was literally going to bite him.

She sat up.

'No, Rory, I didn't mind it the other day. And it was interesting when we paused that shoal of flying fish in mid-flight, and it was exciting when we used it mid parachute-jump, but I do mind a sunset that goes on for Three Damn Hours. OK?'

'Yes,' he said, miserably.

The Super Lucky Romance Camera: Capture the Moment!™ clicked away another minute of perfect, preserved time. It brought up a little image of its advertising on its screen. 'Want to make your precious times last longer? The Super Lucky Romance Camera, with its patented Time Bubble technology will make every minute seem like a day! With a guaranteed reliable Eternity Perpetual cosmic radiation battery, it never needs to be recharged. Take it to the beach! Underwater diving! Even to the top of New York's Ascendancy Tower! It's certified to 2,750 metres above sea level! Your moments are too precious to slip by. Really experience them, with the Super Lucky Romance Camera, invented on Earth in 5044, and now used on over thirty planets, galaxy-wide. Super Lucky Romance Camera: Capture the Moment... For Ever.'

Taking a romantic holiday on fifty-first-century Earth had seemed such a good idea when the Doctor suggested it. Should give them time to get acquainted with the future of their species, he'd said, which was surely the purpose of the whole – he'd waved his hands abstractly – love business anyway? He had a few things to do, he'd come and pick them up in… ohhh, three weeks sound all right?

Three weeks hadn't sounded long enough by half to Rory – they were on future Earth, on holiday, with no monsters chasing them. Surely they'd need more time than that just to get used to driving flying cars and breathing unpolluted air. Not to mention spending time with each other, away from the Doctor. So when the smiling, friendly girl behind the desk – very friendly indeed, to both him and Amy, that seemed to be the way here in 5087 – had said there was a way to prolong their stay as long as they liked, Rory had snapped it up.

That had been six days ago. In external time, that is. But every time they used the Super Lucky Romance Camera, it created a time bubble around them. The way the agent had explained it, time inside the bubble speeded up, so that relatively, things outside the bubble seemed slowed down. Hence, skydiving that seemed to take thirty minutes to reach the ground, scuba diving for hours with fish that glided past in super-slow speed. And now, the sunset. The very, very slow sunset.

Amy kicked at the sand while Rory flicked through the electronic guidebook to Your Vacation on Scenic Earth they'd given him at the tourist information desk. The cities of Earth were all documented, the mountains and lakes and the wonderful smooth beaches of Old Tokyo. Hmmm. He hadn't spotted this section on 'dangers of the beach' before. He started reading. Eight tiny crabs ran over his leg.

'Amy...' he said after a few minutes, 'what does that sign look like to you?'

He pointed at a sign about 200 metres down the beach. Amy peered at it. There were a few small blob-like shapes on the animated sign, moving inside a red circle.

'It'd be a lot easier to see without this bubble in the way!' She kicked at the bubble again.

'Does it look like... a lot of little crabs, to you?'

'Oh yeah! That's what it is!'

In a hollow place by the end of their picnic blanket, thirty tiny jewelled crabs were swarming.

Rory showed Amy the page in the guidebook.

'Mutant reproducing crabs,' it said, 'a beautiful but occasionally tiresome addition to the beach, left over from rampant genetic engineering in the last century. The crabs were created to gnaw out the otherwise indestructible hulks of marine vessels used in the Fifth World War. They live on silica, which makes the beach their natural home, and are generally harmless. However, in an enclosed space, they will begin to reproduce extremely rapidly, their numbers doubling every five minutes. It is important not to erect a tent on a crab nest – if you find that you have done so, dismantle the tent immediately or risk a nasty bite from a swarm of the crustaceans.'

As Amy finished reading, Rory pointed to the little nest of iridescent crabs. They watched it together. Every now and then one of the crabs would grow an extra claw, then two claws, then a lump off its body, and then a whole new crab – conjoined for a second before finally splitting off.

'They're doubling every five minutes?' asked Amy

Rory nodded.

One of the crabs unfolded the shell on the back of its body to reveal a pair of wings, like a ladybird's, and took off into the air.

'They can *fly*?' said Amy.

As if in answer, six or seven more of the creatures took off and began to buzz noisily around the time bubble. One of them hit the edge of the bubble and immediately split into two crabs.

'When is this bubble going to open?!' shouted Amy.

In the nest at the end of the picnic blanket, fifty jewelled crabs had become a hundred. Or two hundred. More were taking off every minute, bumping into the side, doubling. One of them buzzed towards Amy. She batted it away with her arm and shouted with pain – it had left a long laceration.

A swarm was airborne now, flying angrily, buzzing into the walls of the time bubble.

'Rory!' shouted Amy, above the loud annoyed hum, 'when is it going to open?'

'I don't know!' shouted Rory, as the swarm wheeled round and headed for them. Rory picked up the beach umbrella and tried to fend them off. The sharp, silica-shredding claws, instantly ripped the top of it to tatters.

Amy rummaged through her beach bag, at last finding her mobile phone.

'What are you doing?!' Rory shouted.

'I'm calling the Doctor!' said Amy.

'Wait, but… we can…'

The swarm bounced against the side of the bubble again, doubled again.

He'd been about to say they could work this out themselves. It was usually his job to convince Amy of this: she always had some reason to call the Doctor: they'd lost their way, she was too tired to walk back down the hill, the planet was being invaded by giant sponges, the ship was going to explode in an hour…. They had a rule; before she got to call him, they had to talk about it first. But in a situation like this…

'This is supposed to be our *holiday…*' was all Rory managed before the swarm was on him again. He beat them off as best he could with his beach blanket, but it got shredded to pieces. Two more doublings, maybe three, and there wouldn't be a swarm at all any more, just a bubble filled with angry jewelled crabs with nothing to eat but them.

'All right! Call him!'

Amy hadn't even had time to dial the number yet, but there was the sound anyway. It was inside the bubble with them, reverberating and making the trembling walls vibrate.

Vworp, vworp, vworp.

'Did you call him?!' shouted Rory.

The swarm was in the space where the sound was coming from. The crabs confusedly tried to fly upwards to get away from it.

'Maybe he's got a sensor,' she shouted back, 'that tells him when I'm *really terrified.*'

And with a final wheezing groan, the TARDIS materialised. The swarm of jewelled crabs attacked its structure with gusto. Rory wondered how many milliseconds that would keep them occupied.

The door opened.

'Certainly not,' said the Doctor, 'can't go around measuring people's emotional states, that'd be intrusive. Not to mention all the electrodes and implants, very messy. Those things can go badly wrong, remind me never to tell you about the telepathic hair extensions that were all the rage on Cerpris Beta just before the total collapse of their civilisation. Anyway, what was I talking about? Ah yes, that's right, did you have a good three weeks, have you picked up your going home presents, are you ready to leave now?' He suddenly noticed the iridescent creatures covering the shell of his TARDIS, making it look like it had been encrusted with bling by Damian Hirst. 'What are all these crabs? Have you made new friends?'

'Doctor,' said Amy, and hugged him, 'how did you know we were in danger?!'

'In danger from these little things?' said the Doctor. 'They only attack if they're in an enclosed space, perfectly harmless otherwise.' The Doctor reached out to stroke one of the crabs. It nipped his finger, drawing blood.

'Ow!' he said. He looked up and to the sides. 'Ah, we are in an enclosed space. Why did you do that? Very silly of you, didn't you see the warning signs?'

'It... hasn't... been... three... weeks!' said Rory. His arms were covered with scratches from the crabs, but he was damned if he was going to give up any of his precious holiday with Amy.

The Doctor pulled an enormous fob watch from his pocket. Rather disconcertingly, the words 'Rory and Amy Pond' were engraved on the back. He consulted the face.

'Not three weeks, not three weeks? Certainly has been Rory. Time flies when you're having fun, but yes it'll be three weeks just exactly –' he paused, looked at the watch face, waited for a hand to tick over from one number to the next – 'now! Hope you haven't eaten too much jelly and ice cream, try not to be sick on the way home. Well, not home. Probably not. Where shall we go next? Not Cerpris Beta. Never get a haircut there.'

'Doctor!' shouted Amy, trying to interrupt the flow of nonsense. 'It really hasn't been three weeks! It's been six days!'

At that moment, the crabs, apparently deciding en masse that the TARDIS wasn't edible after all, took off noisily from its surface.

'Ah, right,' said the Doctor. 'Time to take down your –' he prodded the side of the bubble – 'whatever this is and let these poor creatures out.'

'We can't,' shouted Amy over the buzzing. 'We're stuck in a time bubble!'

She thrust the pink plastic Super Lucky Romance Camera at the Doctor. He examined it briefly.

'Hmmm, yes. It's only been six days in Earth time, but in your subjective time… three weeks.'

The swarm doubled, overhead. It seethed and roared and raised itself up as high as it could in the bubble and then began to descend, in a noisy, angry, clicking, crustacean sea of very sharp claws.

The Doctor pulled the sonic screwdriver out of his pocket and pointed it at the Camera. The Super Lucky Romance Camera gave a set of musical pings Rory had never heard it make before. And, all at once, the time bubble collapsed – and with it the angry swarm suddenly changed direction, flying skywards, before spreading out across the whole beach. Only a single, harmless jewelled crab was left at Amy's feet.

The Doctor tossed the Camera to Rory: 'Keep that. Useful little thing.'

Rory caught it awkwardly and put it into his pocket. He muttered to Amy: 'Can we just get on with our holiday again, now?'

'Oh!' said the Doctor. 'I've brought you a wedding present. I know it's a bit late, well, you know how it is, one thing and another, time flies when you're saving a planet from evil hair extensions.'

'A present?' said Amy. 'For me? I mean…' she glanced at Rory, 'for us? What is it, Doctor? Is it some kind of fabulous bit of technology, or an ancient jewel or a… Oh, I can't wait, what is it?'

'Far, far better,' said the Doctor, with a smug smile. 'In your species' history, it's probably the most valuable single object there's ever been.'

'What,' said Rory, 'that piece of moon rock they have in that museum in America?'

'Moon rock, pah! I've got piles of stuff in one of the TARDIS basements from when I thought I'd lay crazy paving. No, no, much more expensive than that…'

'The TARDIS has… basements…?'

'Is it the Crown Jewels?' said Amy. 'Did you get us the Crown Jewels for our wedding?'

'Even better.'

The Doctor vanished momentarily and came back holding something behind his back. He pulled it out. 'Ta-da!'

It was a plant, in a pot. Quite a pretty plant. A tulip

with striped, coloured petals. The pot was quite nice too. But still. Amy and Rory looked at each other, and then at the Doctor.

'You brought us a… tulip?' said Rory.

'Doctor, did you just stop off at the local Time Petrol Station and pick up a potted plant before you got here?'

The Doctor's face crumpled. He looked, momentarily, very sad and very old.

'Don't you know what this is? Don't you know that, at the height of its wealth and fame, one bulb of this very rare, very special, practically *unique* tulip would have cost more than… what's the name of the place you keep your outdated mostly ornamental figureheads? The ones that cost all the money in upkeep?'

'Er, the British Museum?' guessed Rory.

'Buckingham Palace! Yes! One single bulb of this glorious variegated tulip would have cost more than Buckingham Palace! Well,' he conceded, 'maybe not that much, maybe not quite that much but close! Someone paid two tons of butter, a thousand pounds of cheese and twelve fat sheep for this! And the rest!'

Rory and Amy stared at the tulip with a little more respect but not much more understanding.

'Honestly, don't you know *anything* about human history?'

Amy blinked.

'I didn't do History GCSE. I did Spanish instead.'

'Right!' said the Doctor, turning on his heel and marching into the TARDIS. 'Come with me!'

They followed, bemused, into the TARDIS console room. Rory brought Amy's beach bag with them. He had a feeling they wouldn't be coming back.

'Bubbles!' shouted the Doctor. 'It's all about bubbles!'

'As in…' Rory ventured, 'I'm forever blowing…'

'No, Rory, as in money. The thing your species is so obsessed with: making it, saving it, borrowing it, spending it. Because money is the best vehicle ever invented for *greed*. Honestly, you know, you really are all just so irrational. You always want to believe you can get something for nothing, that there's some kind of magic power…'

'What, like a raggedy Doctor in a magic box?' said Amy.

'No, not like that, not like that at all. In fact, I am going to take you somewhere that you can see how very not like that it is. Do you see this tulip, Amy?'

Amy looked at the tulip. It was a tulip. It had striped red and yellow petals with frilly edges and a long green stem. A tulip.

'Yes.'

'Do you know why this tulip bulb ended up being worth so much?'

'No.'

'It's because, Amy,' he put his face very close to hers, 'people thought that other people thought it was worth that much. They thought they could sell it for more than they bought it for. They thought that the market for tulip bulbs was so good that prices would keep on rising for ever.'

'But… it's just a flower.'

'That is exactly the point! The point is, you people aren't rational about these things. And that's why…' He typed furiously on a keyboard on the TARDIS console. 'Oh yes, very good, there was an example of just this kind of thinking in your time! We –' he gestured dramatically – 'are going to see a bank collapse!'

'We're going to a bank?' said Rory.

'Not just any bank,' said the Doctor, throwing a lever on the TARDIS console. 'We're going to the scene of the biggest banking collapse your species has ever known! Lexington International Bank!'

With a flourish so dramatic that it spun him around in a circle, the Doctor pinged two buttons, wound a handle and pulled a knob. The central column of the console began to rise and fall. They were off.

'I suppose the holiday's over then,' said Rory.

Chapter 3

London's Square Mile. Here money is conjured and traded, here careers are made and broken, this is the beating heart of capitalism. Along the pavements of the Square Mile stride purposeful women and men with immaculate suits and very short lunch breaks. In the offices of the Square Mile sit people whose days are determined by the movements of lines on a graph. In the boardrooms of the Square Mile are debated the mergers and acquisitions, the divestments and dispensations by which companies and corporations around the world will grow or be dismantled: here decisions are made which will result in a sleepy village turning into a thriving factory town, or a busy industrial city turning into a wasteland of poverty and decay. And nowhere do the women and men stride more purposefully, nowhere are the graphs observed in more minute detail, nowhere are the boardroom debates fiercer or more significant than in the offices of Lexington International Bank.

Here, the atrium is large and the glass sculpture

expressing the motto 'time is money' is enormous. The receptionists are immaculate in identical uniforms. No one would think of striding purposefully through the reception area without carrying a file or two labelled with names that made it very clear how tremendously important they were and how extremely hard they were working.

But nowhere is impregnable. Not even Lexington International Bank.

In the basement of Lexington, there is a loud and busy mailroom. And off the mailroom, there is a maze of dusty corridors and certain damp storerooms which even the mailroom staff rarely visit. And in one of those damp storerooms, the one with the broken photocopier and the plastic mail sacks full of folded up plastic mail sacks, and the copies of misprinted Annual Reports from 1998, in that farthest storeroom there is a noise.

The noise is *vworp, vworp, vworp*.

And then, in the farthest storeroom, there is a blue box with a light on top.

The Doctor opened the TARDIS door and strode out.

'Come on! The air's breathable, the gravity's normal, just my little joke, the air's full of dust actually and the gravity's… well, yes the gravity is normal, although… what are you wearing?'

'Just something I found in the wardrobe room. Coming to a bank, have to dress the part. Do you like it?'

Amy gave a twirl. She was wearing a business suit – a jacket, blouse, short skirt and a pair of glasses.

'But you don't wear glasses,' said the Doctor.

Amy pushed the glasses down her nose slightly and looked over them at him.

'They're just for effect, Doctor. The effect is: I'm very smart and know a lot about numbers, OK? Rory's is worse.'

Rory stumbled out of the TARDIS wearing what was definitely a suit but was also definitely about four sizes too big for him. He looked like his mum had given him his older brother's suit hoping he'd grow into it. If his older brother had been part ogre.

He looked at the Doctor and rolled his eyes. 'It was all I could find.'

The Doctor tried to hide his smirk, and turned on his heel. 'Come along!' he said, 'places to go, people to meet, history to teach! Now… which way, which way…'

He poked his head out of the door of the storeroom, looked left and right and marched out, leading Amy and Rory towards a door opening onto the street outside.

'But,' said Rory, 'isn't this the building? Shouldn't we go back inside to, you know, be in the building we came for?'

'Now, now, Rory,' said the Doctor, 'this is Lexington International Bank! Can't just sneak in the back! Have to be announced at reception! We have to…'

'Please,' said a voice by their feet. 'Please…'

The Doctor stopped. Looked down. Frowned.

Huddled at the side of the building was an old woman. She was sitting under a heating vent, where it was warm. She was wrapped in three or four dirty coats, although she was wearing a pair of expensive-looking high-heeled shoes with red soles. She looked so tired, as though she hadn't slept for days, or weeks. Her long hair was dirty too, and there was a tattered canvas bag next to her which she obviously used as a pillow.

She tugged at the Doctor's coat. Rory was already patting his pockets to find his wallet.

'Please,' she said again, 'can you help me?'

Rory pulled a sheaf of notes out of his wallet and bent down to give them to her. It was funny how, living in the TARDIS and travelling with the Doctor, money began to feel less important, even meaningless. There were seemingly limitless supplies of all kinds of exotic alien currencies piled up in some of the TARDIS's rooms – the Doctor had even told them that one jungle room populated by small pink snail-like creatures was actually a functioning economy he'd picked up on the planet Gigia 8 – but they never found anything much to spend money on, and the things they did and saw couldn't have been bought at any price. He'd brought loads of money, just in case, but now he only carried his wallet out of habit, and this woman needed its contents more than he did.

'Here,' he said, 'have this.' He handed her the notes.

She looked at them, puzzled. She was obviously a bit potty, poor thing.

'Time is money,' she muttered, 'time is money, money is time, you can give me one but you can't give the other.'

Amy looked at Rory with respect. She'd mocked him for bringing along a wallet full of cash. But this was a good thing to do with it. She kissed him on the side of his head, then knelt down, and spoke gently: 'How long have you been here?'

The woman frowned at Amy. 'How long is time?'

she said. 'How long is a day? How long can a day be? Longer than you think!'

Amy and Rory looked at each other, then back at the Doctor.

'I don't know how you bear it,' said the Doctor. 'I don't know how you humans go on bearing this, but somehow you do. That was kind, Rory. Now come along, we've got a bank to investigate.'

'Don't go back in there!' the woman shouted. 'Don't go in there! They'll steal your time! They'll steal it, and you'll never get it back, not never ever.'

The Doctor spun around and knelt down again. 'What did you say? What was that you said about time? Say it again, more slowly this time.'

The old woman stared at the Doctor. Her mouth twisted. She blinked, and scrunched up her face and grimaced. 'Can't remember,' she said. 'My brain is so old. Wait!'

She hoisted the canvas bag onto her lap and rummaged around in it. There was something horrible in there, possibly a gone-off banana and some extremely old fish, judging by the smell. At last, she pulled out a startlingly clean white rectangle of cardboard.

'There!' she said, pressing it into the Doctor's hand. Then, speaking as if by rote, she said: 'Do take my card, it has all my contact details and my secretary will be happy to make an appointment, we're very grateful for your interest in Lexington International Bank.'

Over the Doctor's head, Amy and Rory looked at each other. She was clearly doolally. But the Doctor replied respectfully: 'Thank you Ms, er,' he consulted the card, 'thank you Nadia Montgomery, Head of

Communications and Marketing, that's quite important, thank you so much, we'll be in touch! Won't we?'

Oh yes, nodded Rory and Amy, we certainly will.

As they walked around the building to the front entrance, Amy said: 'What was that about, Doctor?'

'I don't know,' said the Doctor, 'but I have a feeling we're going to find out.'

'I'm the Doctor,' said the Doctor, leaning over the polished granite desk and smiling at the receptionist, 'and these are my two charming friends, Rory and Amy. We're all expected, as I think you'll be able to tell from our credentials, which are here,' he produced the psychic paper and held it up in front of the receptionist's face. 'As you can see we have an absolute right to be in this building and wander around at will, poking our noses into this, examining that, it's all part of our job as our paperwork indicates.'

The receptionist examined the paper and smiled.

'Doctor Schmidt,' she said, warmly. 'The efficiency auditor we've been expecting from Zurich. I'll just call up to tell Ms Laing-Randall that you're here. I know she's eager to talk to you. She'll show you around the building.'

'Yes,' the Doctor leaned back against the desk and grinned. 'That's exactly right.'

'And this must be your assistant,' the receptionist smiled, a shade less warmly, at Amy. 'I'll make up your security passes but…' The Doctor tried to pull the psychic paper out of the receptionist's hands, but Lexington International Bank trains its staff extremely well in security matters, and the receptionist, still smiling brightly, held on tightly. 'Now, let me see, what does it say here about you?' she said, staring hard at Rory.

Rory shuffled uncomfortably in his too-large suit. He didn't look like one of the sharply dressed executives marching through the lobby in search of new meetings to conquer, and the receptionist knew it. She stared at him, then back down at the psychic paper.

'As you'll see,' said the Doctor again, 'like us, he's perfectly entitled to go wherever he pleases in the building, talk to anyone… and if I'm Doctor Schmidt,' he put on a cod Swiss accent, 'ze auditor from Zurich, can I get avay viz zat accent?'

'Not really, Doctor,' said Amy.

'No, no, didn't think so, didn't think it was a good idea at all, but really,' he continued to the receptionist, 'if I'm the incredibly un-Swiss Doctor Schmidt and this is Amy my assistant then Rory must be….'

'Oh yes,' said the receptionist, her face clearing. 'I see it here now. He's the new mailroom boy.'

'Mailroom…?' spluttered Rory.

'Yes, yes,' said the Doctor, 'very good, you go down to the mailroom, Rory. I'm sure there'll be lots of useful things for you to discover. Paperclips, you know, jiffy bags, important staple guns, you never know what could be useful.'

Rory tried to protest, but a helpful security guard was already ushering him through the door marked 'basement'.

'As you can see, Doctor Schmidt,' said Vanessa Laing-Randall, 'we run a tight ship here.'

'Just call me Doctor, everyone does.'

Ms Laing-Randall, immaculate in an extremely expensive-looking suit, stretched one manicured hand out to indicate the glass walls of the internal atrium. She was a woman with the powerful psychological presence of a tank, combined with the sleek grooming of a racing car.

She'd met them in the lobby, followed by her scurrying assistant Jane Blythe, and had taken them on a whirlwind tour of the building: trading rooms and personnel department, management offices, secretaries, private banking. Amy had the impression that, in spite of her politeness, Vanessa rather resented their presence.

'You know the Chancellor of the Exchequer will be giving a speech from this office tomorrow afternoon? Because we are a model for the industry, a model for sustainable growth and commitment to our values,' she was saying to the Doctor. 'I know New York has insisted on audits, but I really don't think we need it. See that sculpture?'

They were looking down on the lobby – the building was circular with a glass roof above the central well. There was an enormous glass sculpture in the centre, reaching up to the eighth floor. It looked like several half-melted candles twisted around each other and fused together, with tendrils and strands reaching up. There was a strange flickering light at its heart. It looked weirdly alive.

'Nice sculpture, yes. Art and money,' said the Doctor, 'money and art. They've gone together since the Medici of course. Banking family. Italian renaissance. Commissioned a lot of art because they thought that was the only way to save their souls from hell. They thought that charging compound interest was a terrible sin, you know. And that God would only forgive them if they used their money to pay for enormous pieces of religious art. Piero de Medici died tragically of Urharborean Plague, but I don't think that was God, more a side effect of some temporal flux caused by Mandragora. Anyway, don't need to go on about that, forget I mentioned it really, what I mean to say is: nice sculpture.'

'That's not just a sculpture,' said Vanessa, 'it's a mission statement. See, the different strands represent the different parts of one's life, and here at Lexington Bank London we believe that each part deserves equal attention. As part of our work-life balance initiative, we...'

She droned on. Amy leaned over the balustrade and looked around the building. Up and down its ten floors, through all the windows, she could see busy bankers working like bees, each in their own little cell. Actually, this place was more like a beehive than anything else. Every little worker with its own allotted job. And Vanessa Laing-Randall wasn't a tank or a sports car, she was a Queen Bee. The whole place was running so efficiently it was hard to believe what the Doctor had told them: that the Bank had taken on too much debt, that it would collapse only a few days from now. 'We won an award last quarter, you know. For our commitment to giving our staff time for family activities, for leisure...' Vanessa Laing-Randall was still giving the Doctor the hard sell.

But maybe she was right. All the workers in the different offices looked so peaceful. Except. Hmm. Directly opposite her, in the glass-walled office that looked out over the central well on the other side, there was a balding middle-aged man who looked in some kind of distress. He'd stood up from his computer, both hands covering his face. A woman ran in from the office next door. He shouted at her – Amy couldn't hear what he said – and she backed away quickly. He turned toward the central well and Amy saw his face. He was middle-aged, quite nice-looking, but full of anger and fear. In desperation, it seemed to Amy, he looked down at his wrist, and what he saw there made him no happier. He fiddled with whatever-it-was on his wrist.

There was no sound, at least none that carried across the atrium. It was just that he crumpled suddenly to the floor and Amy knew, without having to be told, that he was dead.

Chapter 4

They ran round to the opposite side of the atrium as quickly as they could. By the time they got there and found the right office, the man's secretary had already covered his face with a coat. She was standing, shell-shocked, by the body.

'Doctor,' hissed Amy, 'I saw something. I don't know what happened but it was like... he pressed something on his wrist, a watch maybe, and then he just died.'

'Overwork,' said Vanessa Laing-Randall firmly. 'I'm sad to say Doctor Schmidt that, however much we encourage our staff to take breaks, sometimes they just refuse. Isn't that right, Jane?'

Jane Blythe, the assistant, jumped slightly with surprise at being addressed, but recovered her composure enough to blurt out, 'Yes, that's right.' She consulted her smartphone. 'Twenty-three per cent of our staff refused to use up holiday allowance last year. Mr...' she clicked a couple of buttons, 'Brian Edelman here hasn't taken a day's holiday in eighteen months.

That's strictly against our advice, Doctor Schmidt, we've sent him several emails about it.' She noticed they were all staring at her. 'That is, sorry, that's what I've got in my records.'

The Doctor looked down grimly at the dead body.

'Perhaps all those emails got caught in his spam filter. Vicious things, spam filters. I knew one that became sentient once: made a killing holding everyone's emails to ransom. Hmm. Did you say he was looking at his watch?'

The Doctor knelt down and gently pulled away the coat to examine the man's wrists. There was no watch on either of them.

'Well, I thought I saw—'

'You were on the other side of the building, Ms Pond,' said Vanessa. 'I'm sure it was just a nervous gesture.'

'Yeeeees,' said the Doctor. 'Nervous, yes. I wonder how a man in his position, so short of time, ever managed without a watch. Well! In the light of this incident, Vanessa Laing-Randall, Head of the London Office, I think my assistant and I will have to stay a bit longer, conduct a more thorough investigation, wouldn't you say?'

'Oh but,' Jane consulted her smartphone, 'only half a day was scheduled in and…' Vanessa scowled at her. 'Yes of course, absolutely, we can arrange that. Sorry.'

Vanessa put an encouraging hand at the Doctor's back and guided him away from the body of poor Brian Edelman.

'It's a terribly shocking incident. Nothing like this has happened before, Doctor Schmidt. Perhaps you'd like to come out for lunch to get over it? Somewhere comfortable and… well, the Ivy will always find a table for me.'

The Doctor spun on his heel, jerking away from Vanessa's arm.

'Lunch? Lunch is for wimps! I've always wanted to say that, actually I quite like lunch. But we don't need lunch, do we Pond?'

'We…'

'That's right! Lunch is for wimps and we are people of action! So! I think you can go and talk to some managers on the same level as poor Brian Edelman here. I'm sure Jane can arrange that, can't you, Jane, don't bother to answer that, insulting to you to ask really. I think it's vitally important that Amy find out what pressure those middle-managers are under and,' he leaned close to Amy, whispering in her ear so that no one else could hear, 'what kind of watches they wear.' He stood up straight and spoke more loudly: 'I meanwhile will shadow you, Vanessa Laing-Randall, because I rather think that you might be doing something quite interesting. Not to say… dangerous and immoral.'

Vanessa Laing-Randall blinked. 'I've got a meeting with clients from PZP Group, if that's what you mean? I'd hardly call it dangerous.'

'That,' said the Doctor, linking arms with Vanessa, and leaving Amy with Jane, 'is exactly what I do not mean! But come along anyway, to the meeting, no time to lose, eh?'

Down in the mailroom, Rory was also coming face to face with the harsh realities of City life. Mostly those realities were: there was too much to do, there was too little time to do it in, too many people were shouting, and too many of them were shouting at him.

'Come on, Rory,' someone shouted. 'Shift yourself! All those parcels on the noon courier to Rome or you'll be for the chop!'

'Get moving, Rory!' shouted someone else. 'One thousand reports to deliver to every desk in the building in the next hour and no one else to do it!'

'Get over here, Rory!' shouted another angry voice. 'These pallets aren't going to unload themselves, you know!'

Rory sighed. He was in a large basement room with another ten men, all labelling, packing, chatting to delivery drivers, filling out forms. He'd thought this was supposed to be the electronic age but there were still a lot of non-electronic parcels to be picked up or sent round the world. This wasn't the kind of excitement he was used to, travelling with the Doctor. Still, to be honest, this all felt quite a lot safer than usual. Maybe if he could just catch up on the backlog of work...

'Shift yourself, Rory. Chancellor of the Exchequer's giving a speech tomorrow – if we don't get those chairs up to the ground floor, what's anyone going to sit on?'

There was something odd, though. He'd noticed that lots of the packages were coming from just one or two offices. This 'Andrew Brown' was sending out a lot. And another name kept coming up: 'Sameera Jenkins'.

Dean, the stocky man working next to him and constantly whistling in a way that Rory was sure wouldn't get irritating at all if you worked with him for years, was friendly enough.

'D'you notice,' Rory began, 'how many of these

parcels come from Andrew Brown and…'

'Sameera Jenkins?' said Dean. 'Oi, John. Rory wants to know why Brown and Jenkins are making ten times as much work as anyone else in the building.'

John, the short broad-shouldered supervisor, chuckled.

'You're not the only one, Rory my son.'

John and Dean exchanged a look.

Rory waited for them to say more, but they didn't. He knew he was on to something. Maybe he, Rory, could stop this bank collapsing! It wasn't like Amy saving an entire planet from a plague of killer ladybirds (she claimed) or the Doctor saving the whole history of the universe on Tuesday using just a rubber band and a tin of pineapple rings (he'd idly dropped that into a conversation, claiming they couldn't remember it because they'd been caught up in the whole fruit-salad-implosion too), but hey, it'd be something.

So he listened to the conversation around him, hoping to pick something up. John and Dean exchanged gossip about the Bank. Vanessa Laing-Randall, it turned out, had a hairdresser to blow-dry her hair in her office twice a day, morning and afternoon. She was ruthlessly ambitious – had appeared out of nowhere about six months ago, appointed from Hong Kong the rumour was – and workload in the London office had increased steadily since then. Andrew Brown and Sameera Jenkins were known to be arch rivals for a promotion. For a while Sameera had been a dead cert, but recently – no one knew why – Andrew was pulling ahead. Someone else claimed to know, for certain, that one of the most senior men in the building had been on two business trips at the same time – one to Tokyo and one to New York. And no, he didn't mean 'one after the other' – he'd had meetings in Tokyo in the morning, then New York in the afternoon. He must have been on a plane all the time!

Or, thought Rory, he knew one man who could be in Tokyo one minute and New York the next. A suspicion was starting to form in Rory's mind. He couldn't have said what it was any more clearly than 'something weird is going on' – but once you've been around 'something weird' long enough, you start to be able to smell it.

'Does anyone have any idea what's going on with Andrew Brown and Sameera Jenkins?' Rory said.

John and Dean exchanged one of those meaningful looks again.

'If you want to know about that,' said John, 'maybe you need to look in Storeroom F. Just a sec.' The phone next to John's workstation was ringing. He glanced down at it. 'What a surprise, his lordship Andrew Brown on the phone.' He picked up the receiver.

'What's in Storeroom F?' asked Rory. This sounded like the kind of interesting-if-scary thing that could lead to an adventure he could impress Amy with.

Dean nudged Bob, the skinny man standing next to him. 'Our Rory here wants to know about Storeroom F,' said Dean.

A grin spread across Bob's face. 'As it happens,' he said, 'I've got some boxes need to go to Storeroom F. And I need some envelopes from right at the back.'

'It's your lucky day,' said John, finished with his phone call. 'We don't usually let junior staff in there, do we?'

Rory could feel his skin prickling with excitement. There was something in that room, he could feel it.

'I'll go,' he said quickly. 'You don't need to worry about me, I'm trustworthy.'

'That is a load,' said John, pulling a key labelled 'Storeroom F' from his pocket and tossing it to Rory, 'off my mind.'

Rory stood with the trolley full of boxes outside Storeroom F. The door didn't look any different to Storerooms A–E and G–J. Except that it was locked. The others weren't locked – he'd tried some of the handles.

He pulled out the key and unlocked it. As he touched the handle, he felt something like a tiny electric shock but softer, not painful. Probably just static electricity, he told himself. He opened the door. It was dark inside, and the storeroom seemed to go back a long way. Further than the others? Hard to know.

He pushed the trolley into the storeroom and reached for the light switch. As his hand groped, there was that strange sensation again. Like a tingling. And there was a sound in the room too, like a low fluttering hum. With some relief, his hand found the switch. Flicked it. Nothing happened. Great. No light.

He considered for a moment just unloading the trolley in the entrance of the room and forgetting about the envelopes Bob needed. But if he did that they'd all laugh at him. He pulled his mobile phone out of his pocket and pointed the faint glow from the screen around the room. Just enough to see by. He pushed his trolley a few more paces into Storeroom F. Though he hadn't touched it, the door slammed shut behind him.

And there was that fluttering sound again, like a sigh.

Rory found he was breathing rapidly. When had that happened? He wanted to run out of the door and back to the mailroom where everything was light and cheerful. He tried to calm down, breathed deeply, forced himself to scan the room slowly with the faint light from his mobile phone. It was an ordinary storeroom, just like the one they'd left the TARDIS in, he told himself. Look, there was a filing cabinet, there were shelves filled with boxes of printer paper, and… wait, what was that? It was the noise again. Like someone riffling through a phonebook.

He whirled round and pointed his dim light at the place the noise had come from. Something moved, just out of his line of vision, he spun round again, now he couldn't tell which way he'd come into the room and right by his ear something chuckled, a single, mirthless laugh.

He let out a yelp, ran blindly forward, tripped over his own trolley sending boxes flying. The mobile phone flew out of his hand and clattered to the floor. He sprawled on the floor. His heart was hammering in his chest. Something was moving in this room, making that occasional low fluttering noise. He tried to breathe more slowly. He looked around, straining his eyes in the dark to make anything out. He could see the faint glow of his phone a little way away. He crawled towards it. Something plucked at his jacket, as if trying to hold him back. There was the chuckle again, a little further away. The phone light blinked off.

The room was pitch dark again. He could hear movement. Slow, steady movement. Like something blind was groping for him. He reached his hand forward... and with a flood of gratitude closed it around his mobile. He turned on the light, swept it in a broad circle. There was nothing there.

Keeping his back to the wall, he made his way round slowly to the door. He didn't care about the envelopes. He didn't care about anything. He just wanted to get out. He reached down and grasped the handle. Turned it. The door was locked. His heart started to hammer again.

He dialled Amy's number.

'Amy,' he hissed, 'you've got to get down here right now. I'm in Storeroom F. Come quickly. Help me.'

'But I—'

'I'm locked in,' he hissed. 'Help me.'

He swept the light across the room again, and there was the movement. Something was moving by the far files. It wasn't a person, although it was person-shaped. In fact, woman-shaped. In fact, a woman who looked quite a lot like a younger version of the tramp they'd met outside the Bank. But he could tell it wasn't a real person because he could see straight through her. He felt a prickling all over his body.

The see-through woman walked up to a row of books on the back wall. Picked one up. Flicked through it, making a riffling sound. Smiled. And then... vanished. And reappeared right next to him, giving one short chuckle. He jumped, yelped, but she didn't notice. She did the same thing again. Walked to the row of books, flicked through, disappeared.

And then again. And then again.

It was only when she'd done it four or five times that

Rory remembered that he still had the key to the door in his pocket and let himself out.

Trembling, Rory stood at his workstation. John, Dean and Bob were laughing quietly in a corner. In a moment he'd join them and laugh too about the hilarious joke they'd played. Find out what they thought was going on in Storeroom F. But not quite yet. The phone rang, he answered it unthinkingly.

'Hello! Hello, is that the mailroom? It's Andrew Brown.'

He didn't have to say. The high-tech phone system not only brought up Andrew Brown's name on the screen but also a little picture of him.

'Mailroom,' said Rory.

'Now listen, I'm expecting a very urgent package of documents to arrive from Stockholm by courier, and its vital they be brought up as soon as they get here, do you understand?'

Across the room, another man was shouting at John. At least, it must have been another man. Surely.

'Do you have a twin brother, Mr Brown?' said Rory.

'What kind of a ridiculous question is that? I've got one sister if you must know, but I don't see how that's…'

Rory looked down at the little picture next to the name 'Andrew Brown' on his phone, and then back across at the near-hysterical man shouting at Bob.

'And are you wearing a blue tie today, with a…' Rory squinted… 'a splash of egg on it?'

On the other end of the line there was a silence, and then: 'Oh god, yes, there is egg on my tie. Thank you so much for telling me, but how did you…'

Rory stared across the room again and then back down at the telephone. The man with the yellow splash of egg on his blue tie was still shouting – something about a document he needed photocopied urgently about 'tax implications in Delaware'?

'Oh, no reason,' he muttered. 'No reason at all.'

'I didn't ask the reason, I asked…'

But Rory wasn't listening. As Andrew Brown spoke into his ear from his office on the fifth floor, he'd become very sure indeed that Andrew Brown was also standing across from him in the mailroom. Something weird was, indeed, going on.

Chapter 5

'Doctor, what are you doing?'

The Doctor paid no attention. While Rory was trying to get to grips with the challenges of the mailroom, the Doctor was crouching in the corner of the very large, very plush conference room, furnished in mahogany with a carpet so thick that it came over the Doctor's shoes. In the middle of the room was a huge lacquered wooden table. The people sitting around the table were watching with some confusion as the Doctor, sonic screwdriver and a small black knobbly device in his hand, scanned along the edge of the carpet, then up the middle of the windows, then around the drinks cabinet.

'Doctor,' said Vanessa Laing-Randall, 'we're all waiting to start the meeting so if you…'

The Doctor looked at the small black knobbly device, which beeped rapidly and made a grinding noise. He raised his eyebrows. 'Tachyon particles! Loads of them. What year is this again?'

'What…?'

'Yes, what year, hurry please, we haven't got all day or...' the Doctor shook the small black knobbly device, 'maybe we have... maybe we've got much more time than we could possibly use. What year did you say this was?'

'I didn't. It's 2007. But Doctor, we do have to start this meeting now, you see time is running short and...'

'From the look of these readings, time running short isn't the problem at all. But now 2007, 2007... that's very bad news. Shouldn't get this sort of reading unless one of you has a...' He bent his rubbery face into a grimace, then a frown. 'But no, couldn't be that, none of you has enough arms. Excuse me!' he shouted to the puzzled-looking executives around the boardroom table. 'Any of you carrying a temporal inhibitor?'

The executives looked at each other, then back at the Doctor with blank faces.

There was a knock on the door and Vanessa's assistant Jane rushed in. 'The, um, the people from PZP Group are here, Ms Laing-Randall. Shall I show them in?'

Vanessa pursed her lips. The Doctor was waving his knobbly black gizmo around in a circle above his head.

'Doctor,' she said, 'can you sit down and be quiet, just for the next hour, while we win a contract worth £300m?'

'Oh yes,' said the Doctor thoughtfully, 'time is money, mustn't forget that.' He sat, suddenly, in one of the chairs, folded his arms, crossed his legs, in a position of perfect attention.

'Do you know how this works, Doctor? Perhaps you'd like me to give you a run-through of exactly what's going to happen today, and why it's so vitally important that you don't, erm, spend the meeting crouching on the floor?'

'Yes,' said the Doctor, 'why don't you tell me all about money.'

The brief was simple. PZP Group needed a full-service bank to carry them through the next decade and beyond. Well, that was the marketing hype. What it boiled down to were two questions: can you make us money and can you save us money? PZP Group was an industrial company – mining bauxite in South America, processing tungsten in Eastern Europe, constructing engines in Asia – the kinds of boring, sometimes dangerous work without which the whole of Western civilisation would collapse. A big company like that needed a clever bank full of highly educated and crafty people to find wonderful ways to raise money for that new mine in Chile, that new metalworking plant in India. The question was whether Lexington Bank was clever enough.

Vanessa introduced the Doctor to the people around the table. There was Simon, tall, blond, broad-shouldered senior analyst; Rob, slightly shorter senior analyst; Audra, curly-haired senior analyst...

'Don't you have any junior analysts?' the Doctor asked.

'Oh yes, we do,' nodded Audra, seriously, 'but they're not senior enough to come to this meeting.'

And finally Andrew and Sameera, mid-level analysts.

'But they're vying for the top spot, aren't you, Andrew and Sameera?'

Vanessa sounded a bit like a primary school teacher when she said this. Andrew and Sameera both flinched slightly, then put their shoulders back and smiled.

'Oh yes,' said Sameera. 'I know I'm very keen to get that promotion.'

'Yup,' laughed Andrew, a little too heartily. 'And I'm very keen to stop you.'

They both chuckled, the laughter straining the corners of their mouths, and Jane Blythe showed in the clients.

At first, the meeting went well. The clients – three American businesspeople, two men and a woman – enjoyed their tea and made the obligatory little joke about how British people always serve tea. They were relaxed, leaning back in their chairs, admiring the view out of the window onto the glass sculpture far below them.

And the first presentation started pretty well. It was Andrew Brown's turn to present his strategies for PZP Group's next big project, a magnesium facility exporting to Europe. He brought up his colourful PowerPoint presentation with the pie charts he'd spent more time than he really should have both composing and animating. He thought he was holding the room's attention. But then… one of the American businessmen passed a note to the woman. She opened it, nodded, and glanced at the man. Andrew forgot what he was supposed to say next. He stumbled over his words. He ground to a halt.

He stared at the note. The American clients stared at him.

'Is there…' Andrew said at last, 'a problem?'

The American woman smiled very broadly, showing rows of gleaming white teeth.

'No problem, Mr Brown, you go on.' She paused. 'It's only that when Morgan Stanley gave us their pitch their analysis was rather more complex? They'd dealt with the tax implications as well.'

'The tax…?'

'The tax implications in Delaware? Since that's a vital part of the analysis?'

Andrew Brown turned his rictus grin into a smooth smile.

'Oh yes,' he said, 'I've actually prepared a document about that. Just give me a moment and I'll be right back with it.'

It really was a moment, the clients were most impressed. He'd barely left the room, couldn't have had time even to walk down the corridor before he re-entered clutching a pile of warm, newly photocopied documents. He handed them out to the Americans. They flicked through and smiled.

The Doctor looked at Vanessa. 'Very fast, your team,' he said.

'The most efficient in London,' she smiled back.

Simon was next to pitch. His presentation was efficient and effective, marred only slightly by the moment when one of the American men, still faintly smirking, still with an air of friendship, said, 'You know, when we asked Merrill Lynch for their views, they had an expert on International Law standing by.'

'An expert on…' Simon's confidence dribbled away visibly. 'I think we can…'

'Oh,' said Sameera, 'I've asked our senior in-house

lawyer to wait outside for just this sort of question.' She stood up and, looking each of the clients directly in the eye, said, 'I'll just be two minutes.'

She really was just two minutes. Maybe less. As if she'd stepped into the room next door and then come straight back, bringing the in-house lawyer with her.

'Thank you,' he said, 'it was so kind of you waiting all that time with me,' but she shushed him quickly and the pitch went on. Vanessa gave Sameera an impressed nod. Andrew Brown shot her a look of pure loathing. The Doctor raised his eyebrows and said nothing.

Next it was Rob's turn to present his thoughts. Again, the American clients listened very politely, and it was only when he'd got to the very end of his presentation that one of them raised a query.

'But,' said the woman, 'how will technology fit into this? Will we be able to get updates on the project delivered remotely, for example? I'd hate,' she laughed, 'not to be able to check in from my smartphone.'

'We all live on our smartphones,' laughed one of the men, as if this were a hilarious joke.

Spotting Rob's panicky face, Andrew leapt up before Sameera had the chance.

'I was thinking the same thing!' he half-yelped, 'and I've prepared a technical demonstration if you'll bear with me for just a moment.'

It took slightly longer for Andrew Brown to come back into the room this time. About long enough, the Doctor estimated, for him to run down to the end of the corridor, get into the lift, go down one floor and then come back up. Not long enough for him to have, oh, let's say, constructed a working prototype of a field transmitter which would send updates every fifteen minutes to a specially created application which he'd somehow also put onto the smartphones of every client in the room. That would have taken several weeks, not just a few minutes. Although Andrew Brown was looking a bit more tired. And hadn't he been...

'Weren't you wearing a blue tie just now, Andrew? With egg on it?' said the Doctor.

Andrew looked shocked. And frightened. 'I um,' he muttered, 'was I wearing a...'

'I expect he changed it,' said Vanessa, 'didn't you, Andrew?'

'Yes,' said Andrew. 'Now let me show you round this prototype.'

The clients were very impressed. Relaxed, smiling. It was clear that Lexington Bank really went that extra mile. Sameera got up to give her presentation. It was flawless. There were no questions, the clients had no problems. Her last slide was greeted with a riotous round of applause from the whole conference room.

'That was just great,' said one of the American men. 'Awesome.' He grinned at his colleagues. 'Best birthday gift ever.'

Sameera cocked her head to one side. 'It's your birthday?'

'Yeah,' he replied. 'I don't like to make a big deal out of it. Shame there's no cake though, huh?' he joked.

'Oh,' said Sameera. 'No, we've got a cake for you! Just wait here...'

The clients thought she was joking. She wasn't. She left the room for – the Doctor estimated – 12.8 seconds and returned with a huge cake iced with the words

'Happy Birthday Greg' on the top.

'We're a full-service bank,' she smiled.

'You certainly are,' said the Doctor.

'It's all down to the excellent time-management practices I've instituted,' said Vanessa.

'I'm sure it is,' said the Doctor.

And, without warning, he grabbed Vanessa and dragged her out into the corridor.

'So what is going on here, Vanessa Laing-Randall. What on earth is going on here, eh?'

Vanessa gave a wide-eyed look of total innocence. 'I don't know what you mean, Doctor. All that's going on here is excellent business practice at a multinational bank with wide-ranging capabilities and a versatile team who...'

'Don't give me that. Something's going on here and you know exactly what it is.'

'I can promise you, Doctor, I don't.'

Vanessa suddenly became aware that her mousy assistant Jane had followed them out and was staring at them with inquisitive eyes. If the Doctor was about to accuse her of mismanagement, she hardly wanted it to get around all the secretaries in the building.

'Come with me, Doctor,' she said.

They walked along the corridor. In one of the offices, a manager was talking to a pair of besuited salesmen.

'That's right, Mr Blenkinsop, as much as you can use...' one of the salesmen was saying. The Doctor looked at them curiously.

'Now,' said Vanessa, drawing his attention back to her, 'what precisely is it you're accusing me of?'

'Where are you from?' said the Doctor.

'Where am I...?'

'Perfectly simple question, you should be able to give a perfectly simple answer. Where are you from?'

'Chelsea.'

The Doctor took a pace towards Vanessa. She didn't take a pace back; she was made of sterner stuff.

'No really,' he said very quietly. 'No need to lie, it's just you and me, no one else can hear, and you know you can't shock me, no matter what you say. Where are you from?'

Vanessa took a deep breath. 'Just between us?'

'Goes no further.'

'Can't have it getting out.'

'My lips are sealed.'

'You're right,' said Vanessa. 'I'm not really from Chelsea. I'm from Luton.'

The Doctor breathed out sharply through his nostrils. 'That's not what I mean and you know it. Vanessa, Where Is It?'

'Where's what?'

The Doctor stood very close to Vanessa, so close she could feel his hot breath on her cheek as he whispered. 'Where did you get your grubby little hands on a time machine? It must be very crude, whatever it is, so who should I be returning it to?'

Vanessa laughed. 'A time machine! Doctor, don't be absurd, I know we're efficient but we're hardly...'

'All right then, not a time machine, because why would you stay on this planet if you had one? Big company like this, someone might have sold you some black-market technology, calling it...' he waved his hands in the air, 'a Higgs Diverter?'

Vanessa's face remained blank.

'Chrononillium Mega Condenser? Espedarian Back-and-Forth? Raston Warrior Glitch technology?'

Vanessa stared him straight in the eye. 'Doctor,' she said, 'I haven't the faintest idea what you're talking about, but if you're having some kind of fit, maybe you should lie down.'

The Doctor narrowed his eyes and stared hard into her face. 'I'm going to find out what you're up to, you know. Humans using time travel like this – probably without proper shielding, without training, without any hint of bureaucracy?! Have you never even heard of the Blinovitch Limitation Effect?'

'Ahem.' There was a small cough from somewhere below the Doctor's ranting eyeline. He looked down. It was Jane, the secretary. She was holding a piece of cake on a paper plate.

'We thought,' she said, 'you might like some of the birthday cake?'

The Doctor suddenly beamed warmly. 'Certainly would, very kind of you, very kind indeed never say no to a birthday cake – except my own, obviously. If I tried to have a birthday cake the candles would probably set the whole planet on fire, I'm sure you understand.'

'Not really,' Vanessa sniffed as the Doctor tried to cram the whole piece of cake into his mouth in one go.

'Orff Mrrf Gnff,' he said, then chewed hard a few more times, made an enormous gulping motion and swallowed the cake. 'I mean, oh my god, this cake is amazing – I don't know where Sameera got it from, or should I say "when"? But honestly it's... I have to tell Amy. May I?'

The Doctor pulled the smartphone from Jane's hand, and dialled.

'Pond!' he said. 'You have to get up here right now … Yes, of course it's urgent, why would I call you if it wasn't urgent? Come up to the tenth floor right now!'

Chapter 6

Down on the fifth floor, while the Doctor was listening to a pitch meeting and Rory was eavesdropping on mailroom conversation, Amy was supposed to be 'finding out stuff'. What 'stuff' that was wasn't quite clear to her, though.

The Doctor had told her to spend time with Sameera Jenkins, a middle-ranking middle-manager on the middle floor of this tall building. But Sameera – a sweet-faced Asian woman with a Lancashire accent and rock-hard attitude that totally contradicted the impression given by her charming smile – didn't want her around. In fact, Sameera had looked her up and down, said: 'You'd never get away with a skirt that short if you actually worked here, you know,' and walked out. To a meeting, she said.

So Amy did the only thing she could do in those circumstances. She sat in Sameera's chair, checked the coast was clear, and tried looking through the drawers in her desk. She knew what she'd seen in Brian Edelman's office. He'd fiddled with something on his wrist, and then something very nasty indeed had happened to him. If she could just find some evidence that Sameera had one of those bracelets, or whatever, she could take it to the Doctor, the Doctor could solve the whole mystery in one mental leap, and they could all go off to somewhere a bit more interesting than a bank.

The top drawer was open – nothing incriminating in there though, just stationery and receipts. Amy flicked through the receipts idly. How weird. Sameera had bought lunch five times yesterday. At the same sandwich shop, within about two hours. An eating disorder? She didn't look like a woman who ate five lunches a day, but maybe working at a bank was much more energetic than Amy had thought?

The second drawer was open too. Some extremely boring-looking reports labelled 'client guides' and a notepad. Amy looked through the notepad. Every page was labelled with a different date, and had a list of meetings and, for no obvious reason Amy could see, a list of clothing. She looked at today: 'Tuesday, PZP Group, navy suit, cream blouse, pearl earrings, tiny tea stain on left cuff.' Sameera was suffering from some kind of obsessive compulsive disorder.

She tried the third drawer. It was locked. Now, this was looking up. A locked drawer meant secrets, and if the Doctor was involved surely they were scary and exciting secrets, and if they were scary and exciting secrets then she ought to know what they were.

Amy picked up the letter opener from the top of the desk and tried wiggling it in between the second drawer and the third. If she could get the letter opener into the groove in the bar just above the drawer... She knelt down to get a better purchase on the slippery handle. The locking bar was heavy, but for a second she almost had it, and then the knife slid out with a thunk. Try again, get a better angle... She bent over...

'What the hell do you think you're doing?'

Amy stood up abruptly, thumping her head on the desk.

'I...' she said. 'Look, it's not what it looks like...'

Amy couldn't help noticing that Sameera was indeed wearing a navy suit with a cream blouse, pearl earrings and a tiny tea stain on the left cuff.

'It seems to me it's exactly what it looks like, Miss Pond. I don't care who you are and I don't care who sent you, I'm going to call security.'

Sameera reached for the phone. As she stretched out her hand, Amy saw something on her wrist. It was a watch – or something like a watch – a thick black cuff clipped around her arm, with several dials moving at different speeds on the face. And there was something strange about it. It looked like its edges were blurred, as if it was vibrating very fast, or as if it wasn't quite here at all. Amy knew without a moment's thought that she was looking at alien technology. She lunged for Sameera's wrist.

'What's this, Sameera?' she said, 'not something you'd want your bosses to know about I bet...'

'No!' shouted Sameera.

Amy's hand came down heavily on the watch. Underneath her palm she felt one of the buttons on the side of the watch click in. Sameera tried to pull her off, scrabbling at her hand but Amy held on. They fell across the desk, tumbling the telephone and a shower of stationery products to the floor. Sameera's hand was wriggling. She pushed her other hand hard into Amy's neck, forcing her down, and then did something with her leg, taking Amy's knees out from under her. Amy fell backwards, landing heavily on the floor, and Sameera wrenched her wrist out of Amy's hand.

Sameera pressed something on her watch and Amy suddenly felt a moment of tiredness. It was like she got heavier, just for a moment, or slower somehow, and then her body compensated and she was back to normal. She sat up slowly. What she saw frightened her.

It was like there were ghosts in the room – ghosts of her and of Sameera. Fighting. She could see them, hazy, half in and half out of reality, slowly moving and talking and fighting and falling.

'What the hell did you do to me?'

Sameera was staring at her watch. 'No,' she was saying. 'No, it's out of sync. It's…' She pressed something else. The ghosts of Sameera and Amy flickered, then disappeared.

'Do you know karate or something? Because I just saw…' asked Amy, rubbing the back of her head where she'd come down hard on the floor. She'd landed next to the phone. It was off the hook, beeping, and its display was flashing the time: 1.36 p.m.

There was a ghost phone falling down over it, tumbling slowly across the room towards where it was sitting now. Amy put her fingers up and touched the ghost phone. Her hand went through it. It carried on falling.

'Six years of judo,' said Sameera distractedly. 'Black

belt. Just a hobby. No, it can't be broken...' She shook the device on her wrist, and stared at the display. 'It's saying I took double credit? And paid it back asynchronously? Oh no it must mean... it must be because...'

She pulled Amy roughly to her feet, held on to her tightly with her left hand and pressed three buttons on the watch with her right hand, then turned one of the dials back a quarter turn.

Amy felt a slight rushing sensation, a sort of lightness. And the telephone clock on the floor read: 1.21 p.m.

'That's better,' said Sameera. 'Back in sync.' And then, to herself: 'Both of those are on my account, I see.' She smiled bleakly and raised her eyebrows. 'Well, enjoy your fifteen minutes. On the house.'

'You're a time traveller,' said Amy.

Sameera sighed. 'Just for work,' she said at last. 'How did you work it out?'

'I am too,' said Amy. 'Just a hobby.'

Sameera wasn't in any mood to call security any more. In fact, she seemed to be glad of someone to talk to. She unlocked her bottom drawer which, to Amy's annoyance, was just where she kept her sandwiches and biscuits and offered Amy half of her chicken-and-rocket-salad-wrap.

'No thanks,' said Amy.

'Don't you find,' said Sameera, taking a bite and talking through her munches, 'that eating lunch is a real problem? I mean, when to fit it in? I lose track of how many hours I've spent, and what I've already eaten, it all gets out of sync with everyone else. I spend a fortune on sandwiches.'

Amy shook her head. 'I've never really thought about it.'

Sameera took another bite of her sandwich. 'I thought you said you were a time traveller too?'

Amy shrugged. 'I think we use a different method. But how does your... what is that on your wrist, a time-travel watch? How does that work? The Doctor's um, well anyway, I've heard about a thing like a time space-hopper... Is it like that?'

Sameera, visibly relaxed around Amy now that she could talk freely, showed her the watch.

'It's really simple,' she said. 'You just turn this dial here to get more time. Like we just did. Turn it back a quarter of an hour, we're back a quarter of an hour. It's like... Oh, you know when the clocks change? It gets to 2 a.m. and everyone puts their clocks back and suddenly it's 1 a.m. again? It's like that, except it's just for you.'

'And do you always see ghost versions of yourself when you do that?'

Sameera shook her head and opened up a pot of yoghurt. 'That was just because you knocked it. Usually you're very slightly time phased so you can't see yourself. It's always embarrassing, bumping into yourself. That's what they say, anyway.'

'They?'

Sameera ignored the question. 'I suppose I ought to cut back really,' she said, almost to herself. 'But there's so much to get done – you know the Chancellor's giving some speech here tomorrow? We've all had to clear our diaries for that, which has meant triple-meetings today. Plus it's been hard enough to keep up with work as it is. There's this bloke, Andrew Brown – we're up for the same promotion – he's all right, Andrew, nice really, but I want that job, you know?'

Amy nodded.

'Yeah, so for a while I felt like I was definitely going to get it, totally certain but these last few weeks he's been getting ahead of me. I bet he's got one too.'

'One of the… time-travelling watches?' asked Amy.

'Look,' Sameera said through a mouthful of yoghurt, 'if you're a time traveller too, how come you don't know all this? Who do you borrow your time from?'

'Borrow?' said Amy.

Which was the point at which, several floors below her, Rory, locked in a storeroom, decided to call for help.

'Amy,' Rory hissed, 'you've got to get down here right now. I'm in Storeroom F. Come quickly. Help me.'

'But I—'

'I'm locked in,' he hissed, 'help me.'

And then he was gone.

'I have to go,' she said to Sameera. 'My husband's in trouble.'

Her phone started ringing again.

'Pond!' said the Doctor. 'You have to get up here right now!'

'Doctor, I can't, I just promised Rory that I'd go down and… Is it urgent, Doctor?'

'Yes, of course it's urgent, why would I call you if it wasn't urgent? Come up to the tenth floor right now!'

The Doctor hung up the phone.

Amy stared at her mobile, a worried frown on her forehead.

Sameera watched her placidly.

'Tenth floor,' Amy said. 'Got to be the Doctor. I mean, if he needs me for something really urgent then... But then, if it were that urgent, would he have had time to phone? And the Doctor will be fine by himself, but Rory sounds like he's in danger or locked in at least...'

Sameera finished her yoghurt, threw the pot into the bin and put her feet up on the desk.

'Sounds to me,' she said, 'as if you could do with borrowing some time.'

From travelling with the Doctor, Amy was very well aware of the prohibition on going back endless times to revisit the same moment in history trying to angle for a different outcome. Apart from the inherent paradoxes, there are too many beings, entities and sundry monsters interested in the kind of weak spot that generates. But surely, she thought to herself, that kind of thing only applies to travel in the TARDIS? A little watch seemed, well, pretty much harmless.

'Totally harmless,' said Mr Symington.

'We have very reliable safeguards,' said Mr Blenkinsop. 'We'd hate to lose a customer after all!'

Mr Symington and Mr Blenkinsop laughed in unison.

They'd arrived, surprisingly quickly, in answer to a summons from Sameera's watch. And they were thrilled, delighted, eager – as they constantly told her – to give her a watch too. There was something a bit weird about the way they looked. Not just that they were fuzzy at the edges, but each of them had a strange lump on his back, under his jacket. Amy kept trying to get a good look at it, but both resolutely faced towards her, turning as she turned. And besides, they were much more eager to get her using a watch.

'So, how does this work again?' asked Amy, still a little suspicious.

'It's very simple,' said Mr Symington.

'Ludicrously so,' said Mr Blenkinsop.

'A woman of your expertise and intellect will have no trouble grasping it. We simply lend you time. You put the watch on like so –' Mr Symington fastened it round her wrist. It was colder than she'd expected, and heavier. 'And move this dial back to borrow time. And of course press this button to pay it back.'

'Pay it back?'

'Well, of course,' Mr Blenkinsop grinned warmly. 'We can't give our time away, after all! Yes, just press here to pay us back, plus what we think you'll agree is a very reasonable interest charge, just five minutes per hour.'

'Per hour,' agreed Mr Symington.

'The time comes off your lifespan, but after all,' Mr Blenkinsop chuckled, 'are you really going to miss an extra five minutes?'

'It's the sort of time you might spend watching advertisements,' said Mr Symington.

'Blowing your nose.'

'Staring into space.'

Amy hesitated. This definitely felt like the kind of decision she should consult the Doctor about. But if she went up to talk to the Doctor, she wouldn't be able to go and help Rory. And she was late for both of them already. But if she used the watch…

A message came up as if projected by light on the watch's glass face. It was a long message in very tiny print, with big print just at the end saying 'IF YOU ACCEPT THE TERMS AND CONDITIONS, CLICK OK.'

'So just press your thumb here and you're all set,' said Mr Blenkinsop.

'Away you go,' said Mr Symington.

'But what does all this…?' Amy began.

'Oh just do it,' said Sameera. 'No one reads terms and conditions, do they?'

Amy's phone started to ring again. There were two calls coming in at once, the Doctor and Rory.

'Oh all right then!' she said, and pressed OK.

Chapter 7

Amy had to admit, it was exciting.

She didn't feel any different, that was the thing. And it was true, she didn't see any ghost versions of herself, and there were no weird monsters creeping in the cracks in time and space. She just… had more time.

She wound the watch back an hour or so. She was still in Sameera's office. Symington and Blenkinsop were still with her, although Sameera had gone. The clock read 1 p.m.

'Miss Jenkins isn't here yet,' said Mr Blenkinsop.

'It's 1 p.m., Miss Pond – lunch hour is just beginning, and it's yours – all yours.'

Amy frowned at them, still suspicious. 'And you say when I want to pay it back it's just an extra five minutes' interest? Five minutes per hour?'

'Per hour,' echoed Mr Symington, 'that's correct.'

'Just check the terms and conditions if you're uncertain,' said Mr Blenkinsop.

'Now we must be off,' said Mr Symington.

They walked out of the office. Amy followed them but by the time she looked out into the corridor they were gone.

'Is it a crime,' said Amy airily, 'to surprise my husband with a little lunch?'

'No, no,' said Rory, blinking nervously. 'It's just that I, um, I haven't done anything, have I? This isn't the prelude to you telling me that I'm not travelling in the TARDIS any more, is it? Oh god, has the Doctor decided I'm useless, well I am useless, but maybe I'm useless in that useful sort of way? Bait, maybe? Decoy? Attracting attention in the wrong direction? Oh god, I'm not going to have to stay at Lexington Bank for ever, tell me I'm not?'

Amy, unable to think of any other way to stop Rory's hysteria, leaned over and kissed him. For a little while he twitched nervously under her lips, but slowly he relaxed. She sat back.

'I, um,' he said, and fell silent.

'Here,' she said. 'I brought you a sandwich.'

They were sitting in a little courtyard with a fountain, screened from the road by a small garden. Amy had gone to find it, bought the sandwiches, then turned the watch back again so that she could come and get Rory barely ten minutes after he phoned her and only just after he'd realised he could let himself out of Storeroom F after all.

'Ham and cheese! My favourite!'

Amy smiled. This was good. She'd had time to do something nice for him. It wasn't a lot, remembering his favourite sandwich – after all those hundreds of years he'd looked after her in the Pandorica. She found she still remembered that – her memories overlaid on the happier, more real memories. Like a terrible dream, but one she knew hadn't been a dream at all but another kind of truth. In another kind of life, this Rory – happily munching his sandwich, exclaiming with delight at finding a pear at the bottom of the bag because pears are his favourite too, and they're so hard to find in a sandwich shop – in another kind of life, this Rory would have waited and kept guard for her for two thousand years.

She hugged his arm and kissed him on the side of his head as he ate.

'It's because I love you, silly,' she said.

At the end of lunch, Amy dropped Rory back at the mailroom. She thought about suggesting they just leave then. After all, the mystery was basically solved, wasn't it? The reason Rory had seen Andrew Brown in the mailroom at the same time as he was on the phone was because he was using the watch. And Brian Edelman? Well, she hadn't quite worked that out yet – he'd have had to borrow a lot of time for five extra minutes per hour to kill him – but maybe it was just like Vanessa had said: overwork.

Well, she'd go and talk to the Doctor now – that is, an hour ago – find out what was so urgent, show him the watch, which would probably clear everything up, and then they could leave this stupid bank and find somewhere more exciting to explore.

She stood in the Bank's lobby and turned her watch back to 1 p.m. Every time she did it, it was a little thrill. Almost everything stayed the same. A few people changed position, that was all, but it wasn't jerky or frightening, just a slow delicious fade-through as some people faded out and others faded back in. She wondered what it'd look like to wind it back a really long way – twenty or thirty years – and see buildings change. But that'd mean borrowing twenty or thirty years and paying five minutes for each hour and… well, she couldn't quite do the maths, but she was sure she didn't want to end up paying that much interest.

Still, one extra hour couldn't hurt. She turned the watch back again. Again there was the gorgeous melting effect as the people from 1 p.m. transformed into the people from midday. It felt nice physically too – sort of tingly and energising – like she could feel that extra hour of time being put back into her body all in one go. It was like getting an extra hour of sleep, maybe, but all in one second so you could really feel the benefit.

Without really thinking, she did it again. Whoosh! It was 11 a.m., just a bit after the time they'd have landed the TARDIS in the basement. If she got in the lift now, she could get to the top floor before whatever the Doctor had been calling her about had even happened. How impressive would that be?

It was only as she stood in the lift that she started to wonder if the Doctor would actually be that impressed. She stared at herself in the lift's mirrored walls and frowned. There'd probably be a lecture. She could hear it now. 'Messing about with time travel, Amy.' 'Meddling with things that you don't understand, Pond.' 'Do you even know how this watch works?' She rolled her eyes at herself. The Doctor was such a big geek – he didn't understand that not everyone wants to take the back off their computer to find out how it works, most people just want to use it.

She looked at her reflection. When had her hair got that long? When had she even last had a haircut? It was so hard to keep track of these things. And her nails... she usually did them herself but here in the City there must be one of those posh nail bars. And she did deserve a treat... She hit the 'doors open' button and walked back out into the lobby.

She'd meant to go out, get her hair cut and a manicure, and then come right back to the Bank. She really had meant to do that, she reminded herself. The Doctor was waiting for her. That call had sounded really urgent.

Except, there'd been a queue at the nail bar. And the hairdresser had given her a head massage which was so gorgeous she'd completely forgotten the time. And when she was all done, she'd checked the time and somehow it was already 1.30 p.m. And she was late to see the Doctor, again.

She reminded herself it was OK. She could just turn the watch back another hour, and she'd be back to the Bank in loads of time. She turned it back. The street outside the hairdresser shimmered in that beautiful way. The time came back into her body. She felt incredibly alive, excited. And that was when she'd had her big idea.

She wasn't stupid. She added up the number of hours she'd borrowed already. She reckoned it was about five hours. So she'd owe Symington and Blenkinsop about twenty-five minutes off her lifespan. That was no big deal. In fact, what would be a big deal to her? Not an hour. Maybe not even a day. A week. She wouldn't like to end up owing them more than a week. What was she going to do with a week when she was an old granny anyway?

So, how many five minutes in a week? She rooted around in the pockets of her jacket and found an old envelope and a stub of pencil. The envelope wasn't hers – it was addressed 'To the Sontaran Ambassador' – she shrugged. The jacket wasn't hers anyway. She leaned against the wall and did her sums.

So, she'd owe five minutes per hour she borrowed. How many five minutes were there in a week? There were twelve in an hour. So, 12 x 24 hours in a day x 7 days in a week: 2,016. That was how many five-minute periods she'd be happy to end up paying them. And so that was how many hours she'd be happy to borrow: 2,016 hours. Eighty-four days. Nearly three months. That was… exciting.

Of course, she decided, she wouldn't use it all. But there were so many things she could do with the time!

She checked the time: 1 p.m. again. She was late to see the Doctor, again. But it was OK. She'd never be late for anything any more, not really.

She turned the dial on the watch back twenty-four hours. That was a rush. As she watched, the street melted glassily into dawn, across the night, backwards, as the stars rushed across the sky in the wrong direction and then sunset yesterday, and then yesterday evening and then yesterday afternoon. The change was smooth and even, like the day was being poured back. Like time was being poured back into her. And the way it made her feel! She hadn't realised how much energy a whole day was! She felt amazing, like she could do anything. So she hired a car and drove to Leadworth.

Her parents were thrilled to see her, of course. She never got enough of that, never ever. Real Mum, and real Dad. It wasn't that she didn't remember them – she remembered every moment of her upbringing, every school play, every Christmas Eve, every scraped knee and seaside holiday. But she also remembered, somehow overlaid on top of that, what it had been like not to have them there at all. What it had been like to grow up so lonely, only knowing that there ought to be stars and there were no stars, and that a raggedy man in a box would come back for her one day.

So there was nothing better, not really, than spending a night at Mum and Dad's house. Especially a free day, one she'd just borrowed. They were surprised to see her, of course, because wasn't she supposed to be on holiday or something? But she told them there'd been a change of plan. Just for a day. Her mum made her favourite roast beef and her dad showed her his plans for the extension to the garage, and she made them show her all the photos of her childhood again, every single one, just so she could reassure herself it was all where she'd left it.

And she fell asleep under the same old duvet she'd had when she was a kid, with the old Roman soldier models under the bed in their same old box. And when she woke up, the sun was streaming in the window and it was almost midday. Her parents wouldn't like that. Not that they'd be angry exactly, just that her dad would rattle his newspaper and say, 'Up late again, are we, Amelia? Are you getting enough sleep, girl? That Rory keeping you awake too late? Do you want me to have a quiet word?' and the embarrassment would be so cringingly awful that she might experience a single moment of not-bliss in her trip home.

She turned the watch dial back. It was 8 a.m. again. A perfectly respectable time to get up. Plus that gorgeous feeling of the hours peeling away. Her mum was in the garden, hanging up the washing. Downstairs she could hear her dad tinkering with that faulty connection on the washing machine. Hmmm, actually. Amy turned the watch back another couple of hours. The nice tingly feeling washed over her again. She went downstairs and by the time her mum got up, it was she who'd done the washing, hung it up, made breakfast (all right, it was only toast and soft-boiled eggs, but she'd had to wind time back a few times just to stop them burning and hard-boiling, and had had to make a quick dash to the petrol station to buy more eggs), and picked some flowers from the garden for the living room table. She'd even found her dad's spanner and tightened up the loose connection at the back of the washing machine.

She could tell by the looks on her parents' faces that they were impressed. And surprised. Mainly surprised.

She drove back down to London, smiling all the way. As she drove, she kept touching the watch. It was so easy to turn back time. Imagine, she thought, if she did it now while she was driving, the sun would stay just where it was. And it'd feel so nice. She reached over and almost turned the dial when she suddenly wondered what'd happen if, travelling back in time, she hit another car on the motorway. Probably not the best idea. She wondered if they'd mentioned anything about dangers like that in the terms and conditions she hadn't read and pulled over to have a look, but she couldn't make them come up again. Oh well.

Back in London, she planned to go straight to the Bank and rejoin the Doctor. What had it been he wanted to talk to her about again? She couldn't quite remember any more. She suddenly realised why Sameera had had that notebook with details of what she was wearing every day in her drawer. It was so easy to forget exactly the continuity of your days when you could travel back in time as often as you liked.

And suddenly it struck her. *Wearing*. She'd left the business suit she'd found in the TARDIS back in Leadworth, had come back in her own comfy skirt, boots and bright red jumper. She couldn't go into a bank like this! Only one thing for it.

She hit every shop on Oxford Street just as they opened, five hours earlier. She'd never managed to go shopping this early before – without the crush of people, it was just so easy. She turned the watch back to 9 a.m. after every shop, and kept on and on being the first customer. Before she knew it, she had armfuls of bags and was feeling exhausted. Strange – exhausted and it was only 10 a.m.? Ahhhh, she worked it out. She'd turned time back so much she'd been awake for nearly twenty-four hours.

Well, couldn't go and see the Doctor while she was dropping on her feet. Just one more turn. A good long one this time, with that wonderful sensation, and it was last night again. She walked to the nearest, poshest hotel

– all brass signs and polished wood fittings – and using the credit card she and Rory had agreed was just for emergencies, just this once, she checked herself in for the night.

'OK Amy,' she said to herself when she woke up in the big, soft, plump-pillowed, feather-mattressed bed. 'OK, get a grip. Time to go back to the Doctor.'

The watch was still on her wrist. She'd tried to take it off the night before but hadn't been able to manage the clasp somehow.

Her mind rebelled. She couldn't stop thinking of the possibilities. She could use the watch to get something for the Doctor, maybe? What would he like? Or maybe she could go to Lexington Bank a few days ago and leave something for him. That'd be hilarious, just the kind of time-joke he'd like. Or maybe…

She stopped herself. She stared hard at the watch. This was all a bit too easy, wasn't it? She hadn't seen Rory in days, it felt like, and she missed him. Where had all that time gone? She wondered how much time she'd borrowed. It had all blurred together. She took a piece of hotel stationery and a pencil from the bedside table and wrote it all down, as much as she could remember anyway. The hairdresser, the nails, lunch with Rory, Leadworth, Oxford Street, last night… It came to about four days, she thought. Maybe. Ninety-six hours. Five minutes of interest per hour: 480 minutes of interest in total. Enough.

She was still late getting to see the Doctor. She walked from the hotel and misjudged how long it would take.

As she arrived at the Bank, it was 1.20 p.m., and he'd already called her mobile phone. She hadn't answered. She thought about turning the watch back so she could arrive dead on time but she felt a bit sick when she thought of where the last four days had gone. It had been so easy. It shouldn't be that easy to spend four days, surely?

'Pond!' shouted the Doctor as she walked out of the lift, 'You're late. And you haven't tried any of this magnificent cake yet, and you haven't...'

He ground to a halt.

He stared at her.

She knew she didn't look any different. Apart from the haircut and the very slightly different suit but she didn't think he'd notice that.

The Doctor brought his face very close to hers, then looked around her, behind her, then caught her wrist and pushed up her sleeve so he could see the watch.

She didn't know why, but she felt ashamed.

'Oh, Pond,' he said, 'what have you done?'

Chapter 8

'This is bad,' the Doctor said. 'It's very, very bad. I don't see how it could possibly be any worse. How do you get this thing off?'

They were standing in the now-empty conference room. The Doctor was wrestling with the clasps on the inside of her wrist. They looked as if they'd be easy to undo, just several interlocking buckles. But for some reason, his hands slid off every time he tried to open them.

'Protected!' he shouted. 'Woven into your personal time stream, the only way to remove it will be to destroy the central hub where the time is being stored, but where's the hub, where's the hub?'

'Doctor,' Amy said. 'Doctor, why are you panicking?'

'Panicking? I'm not panicking! I'm just very calmly, very rationally, being quite insistent, that we have to get this thing off you.'

'But why?'

'Do you know what this is? No, of course you don't,

why would you, you just let anyone at all put any kind of temporal engineering device on your wrist I suppose. You probably do it all the time. This is a Time Harvester device. It's a parasite. Or, it's a very small element of a parasitic organism. Leave it on there much longer and it'll start sucking the time right out of you and you really wouldn't want that to happen, believe me.'

He was pacing agitatedly, waving his hands in the air and rubbing his forehead.

'Think, Doctor, think,' he muttered to himself.

'But Doctor, it's OK,' Amy said. 'It hasn't taken any time away from me.' She took a deep breath. 'In fact, it's sort of the other way round. It lets me borrow time, Doctor, as much as I want. But,' she added hurriedly, I've only borrowed about four days. The interest is only about eight hours! It's nothing!'

The Doctor stopped pacing.

He turned towards her.

'Say that again,' he said.

'I've only borrowed four days,' she said.

'The other bit.' His face was very grim.

'The interest is only…' she slowed down, 'about eight hours?'

'Did you say interest?'

Amy suddenly felt like crying, and she didn't know why.

'Yes,' she said, and her voice was very small.

The Doctor rested his forehead on hers, just for a moment. He spoke very quietly.

'Oh, Amy,' he said. 'It's very bad, and I don't know how to make it better.'

He pulled at her wrist again, pressed a button or two

on the watch, poked at a little indentation on the face she'd never noticed before. A display came up, projected out of the watch into the air in glowing orange letters.

It read: 'BORROWED TIME TOTAL: 4 DAYS, 3 HOURS.'

'See,' said Amy, wriggling her wrist to try to get out of his grasp, 'that's what I said. Four days. Five minutes interest on the hour, eight hours total. It's fine! I'll pay it back now if you just let me press the...'

She reached for the button that Symington and Blenkinsop had shown her. The 'pay back the time you've borrowed' button. They'd warned her it might make her feel a bit tired, all that time coming off her lifespan in one go, but better that than having the Doctor fussing over her any more.

'No!' shouted the Doctor and wrenched her wrist around so she couldn't reach it.

'Ow, you're hurting me!'

'Not as much as it'll hurt if you try to pay that time back. Look, just look at the interest.'

The display changed.

'INTEREST TERMS: FIVE MINUTES PER HOUR, PER HOUR.'

'That's what I said,' said Amy.

'No, you said five minutes per hour.'

'That's what it says.'

'No!' the Doctor wheeled round and grabbed a magic marker from the table. 'It says five minutes per hour, per hour, totally different thing. If you promise not to touch that watch I'll explain, do you promise not to touch it?'

'Yes.'

'Right! Look.'

He started to draw on the glass wall overlooking the atrium.

'Five minutes per hour, right? So you've borrowed ninety-nine hours, call it a hundred, make the sums easier, five times one hundred is?

'Five hundred,' said Amy, somewhat sullenly.

'That means you'd owe 500 minutes' interest, yes?'

'Yes.'

'No!'

'No?'

'No, because it's not five minutes per hour, it's five minutes per hour, *every hour*.'

'Oh.'

Amy started to have a sinking feeling. The feeling that she'd done something really stupid.

'Doctor, you mean it's been adding five for every hour I've borrowed, every hour since I borrowed it?'

'Yes. But I know what you're thinking, Amy.'

'You do?'

'You're thinking, "Five minutes per hour every hour, that's five times a hundred times a hundred.' He wrote the sum up on the glass wall. 'Which is?'

He was starting to remind her annoyingly of her old maths teacher.

'Erm, 50,000? I owe 50,000 minutes?!'

'Oh, Amy, if only, if only you only owed 50,000 minutes – that'd only be thirty-five days, you could pay that back now and not really notice, might feel a bit sleepy, cup of coffee you'd be fine. Amy. They charge interest on the interest.'

'But it can't be that much more can it, Doctor?'

'Can't be that much more? Can't be that much

more? Don't they teach you anything in school? This is compound interest, interest on the interest.'

He stared at her. She looked back blankly.

'Compound interest, Pond. This is the concept that built banks and empires. This is what means people don't pay off their credit cards. This is the concept that keeps poor people poor and rich people rich on your benighted, glorious planet. It's... look. See this cake?'

He pointed at the enormous cake in the centre of the table which now read 'ppy rthday reg'. The people at the meeting had made a brave attempt to eat it all, but had barely got through a tenth of it.

Amy nodded. 'Yes, I see the cake. I understand cake.'

'Right.' The Doctor cut a slice of cake. The chocolate icing was thick on the top. 'Look at the cake, focus on the cake. The cake, this yellow part, is the hour of time you've borrowed. And the icing is the interest. Get it?'

'Yup.'

'OK, so that's after one hour. Now let's borrow another hour.'

He cut another slice of cake.

'This is your new borrowing. Cake. Plus the interest. Icing. *Plus* you owe an extra slice of icing because you've got two slices of cake, right? Every hour, you have to pay one slice of icing for every slice of cake you've borrowed. Two hours, two slices of icing.'

He made a gentle incision on top of the cake and cut off an extra triangular piece of soft chocolate icing, leaving the cake partly bald.

'Doctor, you're ruining that cake!'

'We'll get another one. Ten. They're delicious. Anyway, look.'

He put the icing, wobbling, chocolately, on top of the second piece of cake.

'Now that's what you owe. Now let's borrow another hour.'

He cut another slice of cake with icing.

'Now the interest.'

He cut two more pieces of rich brown icing and piled them on top of the second piece of cake.

'Careful, Doctor,' said Amy, 'that cake's almost more icing than cake now!'

The Doctor grabbed Amy's shoulders and stared hard into her eyes. 'That,' he said, 'is precisely the point. Let's borrow another hour.'

He cut another piece, and cut three more pieces of icing. He piled up all the extra icing together, with the icing he'd already cut.

'There's a whole extra piece of cake just made of icing,' said Amy.

'Yes,' said the Doctor. 'So now, if you borrow another piece of cake, how many slices of icing will we have to take?'

The Doctor cut another piece.

Amy counted the slices of cake. 'There are five pieces of cake. Five slices of icing.'

'But look at the slice entirely made out of icing.'

'Oh. Right. If that counts as a piece, it's six.'

'So we have to cut an extra slice of icing. Lucky it's a big cake.'

'But six slices of icing is practically a whole extra piece. That means that now, every time I borrow another slice, I end up getting a whole extra slice just made of icing.' She was feeling queasy.

The Doctor nodded slowly.

'You've almost used up the icing on that cake,' said Amy. It was true, the cake was almost completely bald.

'The interest goes up much faster than your actual borrowings. Once an hour, a slice of icing for every hour you've borrowed.'

'That's a lot of icing.'

'That's how compound interest works. Eventually, the icing you have to pay on the icing is thousands of times more than the cake.'

Amy stared at the soft sweet brown mass of icing. She'd never disliked icing before, but she wasn't sure she ever wanted to eat it again now.

'So how much time do I owe? With the compound interest?'

He worked it out for her.

She stared at the number for a long time.

She thought she might faint, or be sick – as if she'd eaten a roomful of icing.

'You must have made a mistake, Doctor.'

He shook his head.

'But I only borrowed four days, Doctor.'

She kept on staring at the number written on the wall.

She owed Symington and Blenkinsop ten years.

'Ten. Years.'

'And even if you don't borrow any more, it's going up by about a year an hour now.'

She didn't scream. She just started clawing and pawing at the watch. She realised she was shaking.

'Get it off me,' she said, 'get it off, get it off, take it off my—'

She picked up a bottle opener from the drinks cabinet, trying to lever the corkscrew under the watch to prise it off. She was bleeding, but she didn't care. She just wanted the thing off her wrist.

'Amy, Amy,' the Doctor was trying to stop her, to get the corkscrew out of her hands before she gouged more of herself with it.

'Is there a problem?' said Mr Symington, from very close behind her.

And then she screamed. Shuddered. Turned. There they were. Suddenly there, from absolutely nowhere.

'We certainly hope there isn't a problem,' said Mr Blenkinsop.

'We certainly hope you weren't trying to remove our extremely expensive chronological asset-management device,' said Mr Symington.

'Because as we're sure you know from your perusal of our terms and conditions...'

'Your extensive perusal of them, as we advised you to do...'

'Attempting to remove a Time Harvester watch is a capital offence.'

'A cap—' Amy managed to squeak.

'Oh yes,' said Mr Symington. 'If you attempt to remove it, your entire remaining lifespan will be forfeit.'

'But you wouldn't be trying to cheat on our little arrangement, would you?'

'A nice girl like you.'

'Oh look, Mr Blenkinsop.' Mr Symington caught Amy's wrist in his cold, slightly moist hand. His teeth suddenly looked bigger than she'd remembered. 'These scratches do seem to indicate that she has been trying.

Bad, bad girl.'

Mr Symington began to smile more and more broadly. His jaw hinged back, far wider than any human person's mouth should have been able to open.

And there were many more teeth in his mouth than there should have been.

Sharp, pointed teeth. To go with his grey skin.

And Amy realised what the lump on Symington and Blenkinsop's back was. It was a fin. Like a shark. Both of them were closing in now, with their shark-like heads and their fins poking through their suits and their enormous, red-as-blood teeth.

Amy looked at the Doctor.

The Doctor looked at her.

'Run!' they both shouted in unison.

They ran.

They burst out of the conference room, the Doctor dragging Amy away from the atrium towards the lifts. Symington and Blenkinsop were in pursuit, their heads clearly visible as shark-like now, their mouths open.

No one in any of the other offices noticed them. Amy realised they must be experiencing the same kind of time-phasing that meant she hadn't bumped into herself while using this stupid watch. Even when Symington jumped over a desk scattering a shower of papers everywhere, the man behind the desk just calmly picked them up as if they'd been blown by a breeze. No one else was going to help them. They were the only people who could even see what they were running from.

'Stop the lift!' Amy shouted as they rounded the corner. There was a lift with an open door. They were going to make it! She felt the hot breath from Mr

Symington on her neck, smelled the disgusting fish-and-blood aroma, put on an extra burst of speed, dragging the Doctor behind her. She grabbed some office chairs as she passed, throwing them behind her to make it harder for Symington and Blenkinsop to follow.

She glanced back. Symington had tripped! Blenkinsop roared at her with his shark-head and dragged Symington to his feet. The Doctor yanked her arm and she fell forward into the lift, hard against his body. She jabbed at the lift-close button, Symington and Blenkinsop were coming and the doors weren't closing and they were nearly here and no one else could see them and—

The Doctor aimed his sonic screwdriver at the lift doors and they closed smoothly.

Just in time. There was a loud BONK and two shark-nose-shaped dents appeared in the lift door. But they were on their way down now. It was only then that Amy noticed they weren't alone in the lift – there was that man she'd seen earlier, Andrew Brown. He stared at the shark-nose dents and at the Doctor and Amy.

'Negotiations,' said the Doctor, 'got a bit heated.'

Andrew Brown smiled nervously and got out at the next floor.

Amy tapped her foot as the lift descended.

'We've got to get Rory,' she said. 'He doesn't know any of this, he won't be safe.'

The Doctor nodded. 'Get Rory, get back to the TARDIS, get out of here, work out how to get that thing off your wrist when we're a thousand years away.'

'Can't they just take the time out of my watch anyway?' said Amy.

The Doctor clasped Amy's wrist and frowned at the device, reading through some small print.

'Hmm. Doesn't look like it. Brilliant legalese – a confiscation of time has to be made in person. And they seem to keep to their contracts. As long as we keep you away from them, they can't take your time.'

'They'll be waiting for us downstairs,' said Amy.

'Sure to be,' said the Doctor, 'with all that time at their disposal.'

'So when we get to the bottom,' said Amy.

The lift pinged. Ground floor. The doors opened.

'Yes,' said the Doctor. 'When I say run…'

Symington and Blenkinsop were waiting in the lobby, their grey-skinned toothy heads weaving from side to side, like carnivorous fish in search of prey. Amy and the Doctor managed to hide behind a crowd of people getting out of another lift and for a moment the two shark-men didn't notice them. When they did, their heads turned at precisely the same moment, a terrifying unblinking stare.

'Run!' shouted the Doctor.

He leapt over the waist-high glass security barrier, Amy followed, screaming at the security guards as they went:

'He's after me! Help, he's after me!'

The four burly security guards in their black uniforms immediately looked behind her. The crowd of people who'd been going about their business stopped walking and started looking to see what was going on. It wasn't much, but they made a few more obstacles for Symington and Blenkinsop to weave round. Amy and the Doctor ran out of the building. Amy grabbed the

Doctor's hand and dragged him towards the little park with the fountain where she and Rory had-had / were-having lunch four-days-ago / right-now.

It was the kind of moment that would have been funny if she hadn't been in imminent danger. She couldn't see the other Amy, but the Doctor and Rory both could. Rory looked at her, and then at his invisible dining companion.

'Amy?' he said. 'But… Amy?' He raised both hands in the familiar 'don't hurt me' gesture. 'This is some time-travel thing, isn't it?'

'Clever,' muttered the Doctor, 'Blinovitch Limitation limitation. Very clever.'

'Yes, time travel,' shouted Amy. 'No time to explain, shark-men!'

She grabbed his hand, and they ran.

As they went, she felt her memories changing. Yes, Rory had suddenly jumped up halfway through lunch and run away. She'd been annoyed.

They circled round the back of the building. They hadn't seen Symington and Blenkinsop for a few minutes. They rested, panting, against the wall.

'Have we lost them, Doctor?'

The Doctor shook his head. 'Totally impossible while you've got that thing on your wrist. If we can just get to the TARDIS, we might be able to…'

'Did you say shark-men, Amy?' said Rory.

'Yes?' said Amy, trying fruitlessly again to undo the straps on her watch.

'What, like those?'

From the other end of the long narrow street, Symington and Blenkinsop had seen them. They started to run, with great loping strides as if they might never tire, and with no one to get in their way.

'Come on!' Amy tugged on Rory's arm.

'No, wait,' said Rory, 'I've got an idea.'

'If they catch up to us, they'll kill me!' said Amy.

'Only if they can reach you,' said Rory, and pulled the pink plastic Super Lucky Romance Camera out of his pocket.

'Oh,' said Amy, 'oh!'

You were supposed to use the Super Lucky Romance Camera on yourself, with the lens turned towards you. But Rory held it the other way round, pointed the lens at Symington and Blenkinsop who were bearing down on them, all grey skin and darting black eyes.

'Say cheese,' he said.

He clicked the camera's button.

The time bubble expanded around Symington and Blenkinsop. They wrestled against it, struggled, gnashed their teeth and snarled, but the bubble kept on closing in around them. With a gentle pinging sound it settled into a bulbous jelly-like sphere around Symington and Blenkinsop. They were trapped.

'Good thinking, Rory,' said the Doctor, obviously impressed.

Rory shrugged, but blushed with pleasure.

Amy poked at the bubble. Inside it, Symington and Blenkinsop looked like they were moving so fast that they were just a blur of pointed teeth and bloody gums.

'Better hurry along now,' said the Doctor. 'It is a Romance Surprise, after all. It might let them out after five minutes.'

Rory nodded and backed away from the time bubble.

He, the Doctor and Amy walked around the corner towards the basement where they'd left the TARDIS.

They all saw them at the same horrifying moment.

Waiting by the door, were Symington and Blenkinsop. Across the road were another pair of Symington and Blenkinsop. Further up the street, towards the main entrance, there they were again. Looking from side to side, in search of prey.

'But…' said Rory. He looked at the Doctor. 'Time travel?'

The Doctor nodded, grim-faced.

'I'm afraid so.'

At the same moment, all three pairs of Symington and Blenkinsop snapped their heads round to stare at them. And then they started to run.

Chapter 9

Rory pulled out his camera, but he knew it was probably hopeless. With so many of the shark-creatures, he'd only be able to form one time bubble before one of the others got them.

Amy began to back away. That was OK. If she ran, that'd give him more time to fend them off. But she wasn't trying to escape. She'd pulled a spanner out of her bag – why did she have a spanner in her bag? – and threw it hard at the nearest Symington, or was it Blenkinsop? The shark-man cried out. There was a gash on his face, in the centre of his forehead. He roared in anger. It hadn't slowed him down at all. All six men roared louder and advanced again.

For a split second Rory saw that each of the Symingtons and Blenkinsops now had a red gash in the centre of their foreheads. That didn't make sense, it didn't…

And then there was a sudden noise. A bright flash, like a firework exploding in the street. And the sound of an old woman shouting. The shark-men all turned to see what was happening. It was the old woman they'd met when they first arrived, the tramp with the smelly old suitcase. She was standing holding her left arm high in the air, waving it around.

Rory saw that there was a watch on her wrist like Amy's. Except it was fizzing, like a roman candle, letting out sparks in intermittent bursts. All the Symingtons and Blenkinsops turned towards the old woman, like sharks scenting blood in the water.

'Over here!' she shouted. 'Over here! Come on, you ugly disgusting lumps, you know you want it!'

She waved her arm above her head and the Symingtons and Blenkinsops stopped pursuing Amy. They turned simultaneously, like an army marching in perfect unison, to run towards the old woman.

'Now!' the Doctor nudged Rory in the ribs. Rory aimed his camera, finding each set of shark-men in the viewfinder and click, click, click. The three pairs of shark-men were frozen in time bubbles.

They all ran towards the old woman, what had her name been, Nadia Montgomery? The card she'd given the Doctor had read 'Head of Marketing' – that had seemed like some kind of weird joke. With everything they'd seen since they got here, it didn't seem so unlikely now.

'That was amazing!' said Rory.

Nadia was rubbing at her wrist. She'd looked full of energy for a minute there, shouting at the monsters, like a young woman, but now she just looked old. Her wrist was raw and sore where the watch was rubbing at it.

Amy looked at her own wrist. 'What happened to yours?'

Nadia rubbed at the sore patch on her wrist. Her watch sparked and fizzed once, a burst of embers reddening the skin further up her arm. She grimaced.

'It hurts,' she said. She held out her arm towards Amy: 'It's broken.'

The Doctor pulled the small black bobbly device out of his pocket and ran it over Nadia's watch. He nodded.

'You're right, Nadia. It is broken. And it must hurt. Look.' He pointed to where a piece of moulding on the side of Nadia's watch was broken open – that was the little hole where the sparks came showering out. 'Something went wrong when they made this one. See the dial?'

Amy couldn't quite look at the dial on Nadia's watch. It was as if she was staring at it through a camera lens, and someone was changing the focus. For a moment the dial would be crystal clear, and then it'd fade into fuzziness again.

'That's why the Symingtons and Blenkinsops can't see you until you call them, isn't it? They home in on the watch, and the watch is changing its position in time all the time.'

Nadia nodded. She looked older now even than five minutes before.

'The sharks,' she said, 'the sharks can't smell me unless I bleed into the water.'

'And it's taking time from you and giving it back randomly.'

Nadia nodded sadly.

'Er, Doctor,' said Rory, 'I think, um…'

He pointed towards one of the bubbles containing a

Symington and Blenkinsop. The bubble was definitely moving more than the others. That was what was supposed to happen – when you only had a few minutes left inside, the time bubble would start to decay. The roaring gnashing teeth moved faster.

'Yes,' said the Doctor. 'Quite right, yes absolutely, must be moving on, well, to the TARDIS I think or... Nadia, could you do me a favour?'

Nadia looked the Doctor in the eye. She was energetic again, not a day over 60. Her stare was clear and firm.

'Can you cure me? Can you make this stop, and give me my time back?'

The Doctor narrowed his mouth. This was obviously a very hard thing to ask.

'Yes,' he said at last. 'Yes I can.'

'All right then,' she said. 'What can I do for you?'

Nadia didn't like to move from her spot outside the Bank. When she was feeling more herself, she thought that this was the only place that she might find out what had happened to her. And when she was feeling so very old, she just didn't want to move at all. And she never went inside. Because that was where she'd put on this watch that led to all this trouble. And that was where the Symingtons and Blenkinsops were.

But she stiffened her sinews and straightened her aching back and, very slowly, creeping very quietly, made her way in through the basement door. She went as quickly as she could, keeping ducking out of sight whenever anyone walked past – no one took any notice of an old tramp outside, but they'd certainly notice if one had penetrated the Bank itself. She came to the door where the Doctor said he wanted her to check. She opened it very quietly.

Inside the small dusty room were hundreds of Symingtons and Blenkinsops. They filled up all the space and the places between the spaces and the space where there was no space. They were folded over onto each other in time – her malfunctioning watch let her see them. There were five or six or seven of them for every one that would have been visible to anyone else. But they didn't see her. They were all turned away, weaving, bobbing their heads, staring at the big blue police box in the corner.

'That's it then,' said the Doctor. 'Given what Nadia's told us, we can't go in there. Too dangerous for Amy, too dangerous all around, especially if they know what the TARDIS is, especially if they can time travel.'

'But couldn't you…' Rory looked behind him nervously. They were marching across Paternoster Square, in front of St Paul's Cathedral. All around them, men and women in expensive suits were eating pricey lunches with pale glasses of costly white wine, with no appearance that anything extremely dangerous was going on at all. Rory couldn't help feeling that at any moment an army of Symingtons or Blenkinsops was going to march down the cathedral steps towards them. They'd only just got away before that time bubble started to decay. 'Couldn't you, just, you know, run through, open the TARDIS, go and pick up Amy, get out?'

The Doctor was walking faster now, his long legs striding north past identical-looking grey stone office buildings. Rory glanced into a window. He could have sworn he saw a Symington in there. Or maybe a Blenkinsop. Surely he was imagining it.

'No, Rory,' the Doctor shouted. 'You really do need to get the fundamentals of time travel into your head. If we run in and try to get to the TARDIS, they only have to travel back a few minutes to be ready for us. You really shouldn't do that, of course, goodness knows what it's doing to the temporal superstructure of this planet but— Wait, of course. Of course!'

'What's that, Doctor?' Amy was striding along beside the Doctor. Rory didn't understand why, given that he wasn't any shorter than either of them, but he was always the one not quite keeping up. He quickened his pace.

The Doctor stopped suddenly. Rory walked into him.

'Sorry, sorry,' said Rory, but the Doctor didn't notice. He smacked his palm against his forehead.

'Of course,' said the Doctor again, spinning on his heel. 'Of course, time travel!'

Amy and Rory looked at each other in bewilderment, then back at the Doctor.

'Did you see what happened, when you threw that spanner at one of the Symingtons? No of course you didn't, of course not – you were frightened, you were running for your life. It was just a split second.'

'I saw,' said Rory. 'They all suddenly had a wound on their foreheads.'

'Yes! Brilliant! Why do I always underestimate you, Rory, you're brilliant! Now, tell me why that happened.'

'I, um...'

'Yes I see, not quite there yet, well why should you be? It's because...' the Doctor spread his arms very wide as if revealing the finale to a magic trick, 'they're all the same person!'

Amy and Rory looked at each other again. Rory wondered if Amy had understood what the Doctor was talking about. He didn't want to admit that he hadn't, especially if Amy had already got it.

'What are you talking about, Doctor?' asked Amy.

'They're the same creature!' said the Doctor. 'Folded back on themselves in time. Do you remember how they all turned their heads to look at us in unison? That's why they all saw us at the same moment! When one of them sees, all the rest of them – all the ones that are later in the timeline, that is – remember seeing.'

'Does that mean,' said Rory, 'that it's very, very bad if one of them spots us?'

'Yes, Rory,' said the Doctor. 'It's positively catastrophic!' he spat out gleefully. 'If one of them sees us then all the others that come later in the time stream instantly know where we are, because they remember it in their own past. Clever, isn't it?'

Rory pointed down a little side street off to the left. He knew he'd been right about what he'd seen in that office building. Walking almost casually, its head cocked to one side, baring its diamond-shaped teeth just a fraction, was a Blenkinsop.

'Run!' shouted the Doctor.

They ran through the streets of the City of London, along office-building-lined Newgate Street, where Rory was sure he saw a Symington or a Blenkinsop in every window, across Holborn Viaduct then, doubling back, along Smithfield Street and round the medieval buildings of Cloth Fair and Rising Sun Court.

'Amazing isn't it, the City?' shouted the Doctor.

Rory glanced behind him. The Blenkinsop wasn't gaining on them, but it wasn't losing much ground either.

The Doctor wasn't out of breath at all. That's what you got for having two hearts, Rory guessed.

'All these buildings,' he continued. 'All different periods of history. Did you know this part of London has been continually inhabited for more than two thousand years? No, I suppose not since neither of you took History. It's up to me to teach you, I suppose. See that over there?' He pointed to a quite modern-looking building with leaded windows and cream-coloured plaster arches at the base. 'Oldest house in London that is. I was there when they laid the foundation stone. Really nice bloke – Tom something – shame what happened with the Alicagorians later. Ah well, at least the house is still here.'

'All very interesting, Doctor,' Amy panted, 'but maybe when we're in less danger of *being eaten*?'

The Doctor was leading them in a wide circle. They passed more offices and sandwich shops, then took a sharp right at Barbican station.

'Oh, now I have to show you this,' said the Doctor, as they ran down another street and came to a small park screened from the road by trees. 'Postman's Park, have you been here before? Amazing place! All these plaques,' he pointed at a row of tiles underneath an awning, 'are for ordinary people who sacrificed themselves to help others.'

He stopped suddenly in front of the memorial.

'Amazing,' he said. 'You get so little time, and yet you

use it to help other people.'

'Yes this is all interesting,' said Rory, 'but Doctor, *shark-men are coming*!'

Three Symingtons and a Blenkinsop rounded the corner, teeth bared, eyes rolling.

'Oh... yes,' said the Doctor. 'Well, now we're not anywhere too crowded...'

He grabbed Amy's wrist and aimed the sonic screwdriver at it.

'Er, what are you doing, Doctor?' asked Amy.

'Voiding the warranty.'

He pressed three buttons on Amy's watch in quick succession, and aimed another burst of his sonic screwdriver. The watch let off a burst of sparks, which travelled upwards into the air. As Rory watched, the sparks turned, directing themselves back in the direction of the Bank. The Symingtons and Blenkinsops stopped dead in their tracks, looked around in puzzlement, then, as if in answer to a call from behind them, all turned around and ran purposefully in the opposite direction, away from the Doctor, Rory and Amy.

'Are we safe now, Doctor?' asked Amy.

The Doctor opened his eyes very wide. 'No,' he said, 'not at all. We're not going to be safe until the very last one, or in fact the very first one of those creatures is off your world. But if you mean "Are they going to try to kill us in the next twenty minutes?" safe, then yes, we're safe.'

'So, um,' said Amy, staring at her watch, which had a couple of residual sparks adhering to the face, 'what did you do?'

'I did to your watch in a controlled way what happened to Nadia's in an uncontrolled way, do you see?'

'No.'

'No reason you should, very complicated temporal physics, have I mentioned I'm a genius? I'll try to make it very simple. A bit of your time is now back at the Bank, so that is where the Symingtons and Blenkinsops will think you are, at least for a while. Now do you understand?'

'No.'

'We're safe for the moment,' said the Doctor, speaking very slowly 'but we have to identify whichever one is first in the time loop possibly by some kind of regressive temporal analysis to prevent the spread of the Time Harvester watches in the first place, plus we need to find the containment device where they're storing the time – very tricky business, time storage, get one of your parameters wrong and your storage tank will age ten million years overnight – we'll need to find it and deactivate it. Do you understand that?'

'Do you mean' said Amy, 'that we have to get rid of the shark-men and get everyone's time back?'

'Yes,' said the Doctor, pouting a little.

'That,' said Amy, 'I can get behind.'

Chapter 10

'Firstly,' said the Doctor, 'we need a friend in the Bank.'

'What about Nadia?' said Amy, 'she can go in there for us any time, look around, find things out.'

The Doctor shook his head. 'She's too unstable, temporally. We've seen her age and get younger by twenty years in thirty seconds. Plus she's doing something important for me back there already.'

Rory and Amy exchanged a look.

'You didn't tell us that Nadia was doing anything important?'

'She's keeping an eye on the TARDIS. Most important thing of all. Anyway, we need someone who can go into the Bank without arousing anyone's suspicion – Symington, Blenkinsop or human – and look at files, find out what's going on and who first brought those watches to the Bank.'

'What about—' began Rory.

'Just a moment, Rory, I'm thinking. We need someone

who's heavily involved in this already, who might have borrowed more than they realise...'

'But I was going to say—' said Rory.

'Just a minute, Rory, I have to think this through. We need someone we can trust, just an ordinary bloke, an everyday, normal person who's in over their head, and—'

'Andrew Brown!' shouted Rory.

'Calm down, Rory, no need to shout.'

'Andrew Brown,' said Rory again, a shade more calmly. 'He's borrowed loads of time. I've seen him in three different places at the same time in the Bank. He's probably up to his neck in debt and...'

'Well, why didn't you say so? Come on, let's go and find him. At home's best. We don't want to go back to the Bank for the moment.'

'But how will we know where he lives, Doctor?' asked Amy. She scratched at the watch strap on her wrist. It was beginning to irritate her skin, just like Nadia's did.

'Directory enquiries,' said the Doctor.

Nadia dragged her bag along the storeroom corridors, looking for somewhere quiet to wait. The TARDIS was back in one of the large unused basement rooms at the end of the corridor. The Symingtons and Blenkinsops were fascinated by it, but none of their clawing and pawing was getting them in. Still, she needed to make sure they didn't try anything more extreme – the Doctor had told her that the TARDIS's Hostile Action Displacement System would stop them actually getting in, but would also mean the whole box moved somewhere else – and he preferred not to have to go hunting for it. 'Very boring,' he said, 'not to mention incredibly embarrassing. Like losing your car in a car park. If I remembered to set it.'

So, she had a watching brief. She could do that. She pulled her bag into a storeroom whose door was unexpectedly propped open by an overturned mailroom trolley, wedged the door slightly open with a few files and sat in the dark. Once an hour, she'd venture out to see if anything had happened to the TARDIS. Other than that, she'd wait.

The Doctor was trying to remember a number.

'112358e963i? Or did it have something to do with Pi?'

'If you want directory enquiries, Doctor,' said Amy, 'there are loads of numbers. They all start 118 something.'

'That's not what I mean, not what I mean at all,' snapped the Doctor, 'there's a new galactic system that's just been introduced, trial run, fun to give it a go, let's have your phone.'

Amy, with a dubious expression, handed him her mobile phone. He dialled about 25 numbers and made a series of high-pitched whines into the handset. Amy raised an eyebrow.

'It's connecting! I'll put it on speakerphone! Isn't this fun?'

'Galactic Enquiries,' said a woman with a low buzzing voice, 'which name do you require?'

'What was the name again, Rory?' said the Doctor.

'Um, Andrew Brown. London,' said Rory.

'Searching for you.'

'There are going to be loads of Andrew Browns,

though, aren't there?' said Rory.

'Don't worry,' whispered the Doctor, 'they've got a system for dealing with it! That's what they say, anyway.'

'I've found 2,361 Andrew Browns living in the Greater London area,' the voice said smoothly, 'including several species and organisations with similar names, for example the Ah N'Drubrn Clan of Warrior Molluscs currently residing in the Thames and the End, Rue, Burn Doomsday Cult intending to destroy the city in a little over 271 days from now.'

'I told you she wouldn't be able to— wait, what was that? Destroy the city?'

'We'll come back for them later, Rory. Or, hmm, actually I think I've dealt with them earlier. Later. I will have dealt with them earlier later already. Why don't human languages have tenses for these things? If we were speaking Old High Gallifreyan, you'd have understood me before I started talking. Tell me,' he addressed the woman on the phone, 'what is the best way to find the Andrew Brown we're looking for?'

'I will ask you a few brief questions,' she said, 'to find your party. Is your party human?'

The Doctor turned to Rory. 'Is he human?'

Rory raised both eyebrows.

'Yup, human, yup.'

'Male or female?'

The Doctor looked at Rory. Rory looked back.

'Male,' said the Doctor.

'Hmmm.' The woman paused. 'Brown hair, brown eyes, bit of a bump on his nose?'

'Umm,' said Rory, 'not a bump exactly but his nose is quite…'

'Quite a long nose?'

'Yes!' said Rory.

'And does he have an air of vague discomfort? As if he were...'

'As if he's constantly late for something! Yes!' shouted Rory.

'I've narrowed it down to fifteen possibilities for you. Is he a fan of snooker, do you know?'

'No idea.'

'Is his mother's name Margaret?'

'How am I supposed to know these things?' Rory said. 'I know where he works if that helps: Lexington Bank.'

'Sorry, we don't hold that information.'

Rory rolled his eyes.

The Doctor whispered, 'I did hear the system was at a very experimental stage...'

'Now this is a bit of a long shot,' said the woman on the phone, 'but does he have a stain on his tie today?'

'Yes!' said Rory. 'Yes, it's—'

'Custard?'

'Egg!'

'Very good,' said the buzzing woman. 'I've got your man. Displaying his address for you now.'

The screen flashed up a message and then went dark.

'She didn't even wish us a nice day,' said the Doctor.

'How do we know he'll even be here, Doctor?' said Amy. 'It is a workday, after all.'

They were walking down a suburban street in North London, looking for Andrew Brown's flat. It was late afternoon. Amy wondered idly how many times she'd lived this particular hour already. She felt that she'd seen the sun getting low on the horizon surrounded by pink-streaked clouds like that quite a few times now.

'Yeah,' said Rory, 'even if he's been using the watch a lot to get ahead at work, surely he'd only use it when he's actually at the office.'

'Yeah,' said Amy, 'no one would be so stupid as to use something like that for fun, would they?'

Rory didn't know what she'd done. There hadn't been any point telling him. The Doctor would fix it and then it'd all be fine and there'd be no reason for him ever to know.

They rounded the corner. Amy's voice dwindled to nothing.

'Yeah,' said Rory, 'I think he's here.'

There was no need for them to wonder which was Andrew Brown's flat. He was everywhere on it, and in it. There was an Andrew Brown on a ladder painting the window frames. And an Andrew Brown trimming the hedge. An Andrew Brown was taking out the rubbish, and another Andrew Brown was cleaning the car. Inside the ground floor flat, they could see an Andrew Brown talking on the phone. And one cooking in the kitchen. And another working at the computer. And another playing a video game. One was just walking up the path to the front door as another was coming out in a rush. They were all going about their business apparently totally unaware of the others' presences, but managing never quite to bump into each other, as if they were in a well-choreographed ballet.

'How do his neighbours not notice?' muttered Amy. She was thinking of her parents' house in Leadworth.

There was something really horrible about the way the house covered in Andrew Browns looked. As if he'd stopped being a person and was more like an infestation. She hated the idea that she'd made her parents' house look like that. That she was doing it right now, at the same time that she was here.

'Oh, British people are very polite, you know. Don't upset the neighbours, don't complain if they make lots of noise, try not to notice if they're clearly travelling in time. Stiff upper lip, Pond! Excuse me?'

Several of the Andrew Browns turned round at the same time. Amy wondered if they now all remembered seeing the Doctor at various different points across the past few days. It must get boring, mustn't it? It had been quite fun while she'd been living the same day over and over, but now she came to think of it... didn't Andrew Brown want to see what was going to happen tomorrow?

The Andrew Brown washing the car squinted at them, then his face cleared into a smile: 'Hang on, I know you from the Bank, don't I? Doctor Schmidt? The expert from Zurich? How can I help you?'

The Andrew Browns went back to what they were doing.

'Clever,' said the Doctor. 'You must be the earliest, am I right? So the others remember that you talked to me, so they don't have to talk to you.'

'I'm sorry, I don't quite understand,' said Andrew.

'Ah yes,' said the Doctor. 'Tricky thing, time travel. Especially if you're not biologically designed for it. I expect they've got some gizmo in that device on your wrist so you don't have to worry about it yourself. I tried something like that myself once with the TARDIS psychic circuits when I kept bumping into myself – got into a terrible mess, no one could see my reflection for weeks, gave the people of Transylvania quite a fright. Let me just take a look.'

The Doctor lunged for Andrew's wrist, all floppy limbs and clownish gestures and nonsense-talking. Andrew, more amused than frightened, let him look. The Doctor held Andrew's watch up to his ear, then held the wrist between thumb and forefinger.

'How much have you borrowed, Andrew?'

'Excuse me?'

'We haven't got time for this, Andrew, at least you certainly haven't. Mr Symington and Mr Blenkinsop, how much time have you borrowed from them?'

'I, um, I don't know what you're talking about.'

'I think you do, Andrew, I think you really do. How much time have you borrowed? It's important. Really, really important.'

Andrew ran a hand through his hair. He stared at the Doctor and then glanced at Amy who smiled winningly. Andrew smiled back. He took a deep breath. 'A few days? Not more than a week. And I try to pay it back when I can, only…'

'Yes, it feels nasty to pay it back, nice to borrow it, totally understand. I think you've borrowed more than you reckon, Andrew.'

'Well, I, er, I don't know, maybe ten days? A couple of weeks?'

'I think it's more than that, Andrew.'

The Doctor whipped the sonic screwdriver out of his pocket and made a few passes with it over the watch.

'Nothing in my right hand, nothing in my left hand… well, all right, a sonic screwdriver in my left hand. And… alakazam!'

A glowing display hovered in the air in front of the watch, just like the one the Doctor had made appear from Amy's watch in the boardroom.

'Wow,' said Rory.

'Oh,' said Amy. 'That's…'

'BORROWED TIME TOTAL SINCE LAST REPAYMENT: 9 DAYS, 1 HOUR. INTEREST TERMS: 5 MINUTES PER HOUR, PER HOUR. TOTAL TIME OWED: 55,000 YEARS.'

Andrew Brown sat down with a plonk on his driveway. All the other Andrew Browns around the house vanished, one after the other. The window frame went back to being unpainted, the cooking smells vanished from the kitchen.

'Ah, I see you'll decide not to borrow any more, very wise given you owe them more than the lifespan of five hundred people. Hang on.' The Doctor cocked his head to one side. 'You owe them more than you can possibly pay back…'

'I think that's obvious, Doctor.' Amy crouched down and put a hand on Andrew's shoulder. 'It's going to be OK,' she told him. 'The Doctor will figure it out.'

'No, but,' the Doctor was emphatic, 'he owes more than he can ever possibly pay back. They've lent him more than he could ever, ever pay back. That's…'

'It's criminal, Doctor,' said Amy, her eyes suddenly wet with tears.

'It's interesting,' said the Doctor. 'Very interesting… It almost suggests that—'

'But I don't understand,' Andrew interrupted. 'Surely there should be some warning system? Something to tell me when I'd…' An angry look came over his face. 'Look, how do I know you're even telling the truth? I don't know what you did to my watch, this could all be lies! I only borrowed a few days!'

'If you don't believe me,' said the Doctor nonchalantly, 'just pay it back. They've loaned you more than you could ever, ever pay back that's very—'

'No!' shouted Amy. She turned Andrew's face to look at her. 'I know it sounds bad, and I know it sounds crazy,' she said, 'but you can trust the Doctor, just not when he's…' she looked up at the Doctor who was muttering numbers under his breath, apparently doing mental arithmetic, 'just not when he's distracted, OK? But you can trust him. We'll figure this out.'

'I don't see why I should believe any of this,' Andrew said again. 'It sounds made up.'

'Denial,' said the Doctor. 'Classic, my old friend Siggy Freud used to tell me that all the time. "Vell, Doctor," he'd say, "ven confronted vis ze unbelievable, ze human brain goes into shock!"'

Amy held Andrew Brown's hand. 'You have to believe us,' she said. 'We're telling the truth.'

Andrew stood up shakily. 'If you're telling the truth,' he said, 'then if I instruct the watch to pay back one per cent of one per cent of what I owe, I should pay back, what, five years?'

'Five and a half,' said the Doctor.

'Right then,' said Andrew. He brought up a menu on the watch and clicked a button.

'Make sure you get the decimal point in the right

place,' said the Doctor.

Andrew moved a dial fractionally, and pressed another button.

He sank to his knees with a groan.

A streak of grey appeared in his hair, and wrinkles deepened on his forehead.

He looked at himself in his car's wing mirror.

Rory and Amy watched him, not daring to speak.

Even the Doctor was paying attention now.

'My god,' said Andrew. His voice was a croak. 'I'm… you're right. But… everyone's using the watches.' He looked up in horror. 'How can we stop this?'

'That, Andrew, is where you come in,' said the Doctor, helping him to his feet with an arm. 'And don't worry, you don't have to call me God.'

Chapter 11

'It's a lot to take in, that's all I'm saying.' Andrew Brown was sitting in an armchair in his living room with his head in his hands. Amy nodded sympathetically.

'So there are... aliens?' asked Andrew.

'What did you—' began Rory. 'I mean, sorry, but who did you think had given you a watch that lets you travel in time?'

Andrew shrugged. 'I thought maybe some... government programme? Military technology? Something Russian? Maybe what they're doing with the Large Hadron Collider.'

'You'd need a very large collider indeed to even start to find the particles that can do what that watch can do,' said the Doctor acidly.

Andrew looked up at the three people gathered around him. 'And you're all... aliens?'

Rory shook his head vigorously. 'No, no, definitely not, only one of us is an alien and you see...'

Andrew pointed at Amy. 'So you're the alien!'

'I know she can seem a bit strange at times –' Amy raised her eyebrows and gave the Doctor a very hard stare – 'but no. Look. It doesn't matter who's an alien, who's not an alien, who happens to have two hearts and who'd prefer that they were not revealed to the authorities…' The Doctor knelt down in front of Andrew. 'What matters is, we need your help. The Symingtons and Blenkinsops—'

'The aliens,' said Andrew.

'Yes, the aliens. The other aliens. The Symington and Blenkinsop aliens are doing something with all the time they're siphoning off people. I've done all the checking I can without access to my TAR– without my proper equipment, and I don't think they're taking it off-planet. Which would make sense. Very volatile substance, time. Hard to transport. So they must be storing it somewhere on Earth. Probably very nearby. Probably, we think, somewhere in the Bank!'

'So we think you can help us.' Amy flared her nostrils and gave Andrew a look somewhere between seduction and interrogation.

'We need you to look around the Bank,' continued the Doctor, 'for a storage system. It'd be pretty large, probably central, and…'

'No,' said Andrew.

'No?' said the Doctor, 'I don't think that you quite understand the gravity of the situation. This isn't some kind of worldwide banking crisis, you know, there's not going to be any bailout this time.'

'I mean, no, it's not in the Bank,' said Andrew. 'I think I know where it is.'

*

The Symingtons and Blenkinsops were on the move in Lexington Bank's basement. They'd tried prising the door open in the usual ways, and with some unusual devices Nadia had never seen before. Now they were muttering about 'talking to the head'.

It was strange to walk among them and not be seen. She'd realised maybe a month earlier that they sometimes couldn't see her. One of the Symingtons had tripped over her, grazed his forehead – she'd seen a similar graze on the heads of several others for a couple of days afterwards – and looked round, unable to see what he'd fallen over. The effect only lasted for a few seconds, then the watch did something and he saw her again, snarled, walked on. It had been lasting longer and longer, recently.

But this feeling was new – seeking them out. And observing them, trying to get to know them. They didn't talk much, that was peculiar. When they did, it was almost interchangeable which of them spoke. It wasn't just that they finished each other's sentences; sometimes they took only a few words each in an emerging thought, or seemed to be having half the conversation almost telepathically.

'We should,' said one.

'Yes, possibly,' said another.

'Bring it, then,' said a third, 'and we'll…'

'Be able to break into the machine,' finished a fourth.

Nadia, in the centre, unseen, listened and waited.

Andrew flipped through another folder. There were nine or ten of them stacked up around him: large lever-arch document folders, filled with paper printouts.

'You see, I've been using all my extra time wisely,' said Andrew.

'Yeah,' said Rory, 'all 55,000 years of it. That was a wise choice. Didn't you want to do anything else with your life but work, mate?'

Andrew looked at Rory. He had had dreams once, he was sure of it. Not just things that let him relax after a day's work, but interests, hobbies, passions. Bands he wanted to see play so much it ached. Music he wanted to make himself. There was a guitar in the loft, and he'd always thought… well, he wasn't much of a musician himself, but he'd enjoyed teaching other people to play and… it was a really long time ago now.

He shrugged. 'I don't know,' he said.

Amy tried to look interested in the folders. 'I'm sure it seemed like a good idea at the time, didn't it, Andrew?'

'I shouldn't really have done it, but I've taken a look through the earning and spending reports – I was going to suggest where we could tighten up our budget, you see.'

'Oh yes, that is a good use of 55,000 years,' said Rory.

'Ah! Here it is!'

Andrew triumphantly tore a sheet out of his folder. It was an invoice from a company called Little Green Storage for £454,909.

'There's one of those every month,' said Andrew. 'They're paid out of an anonymous account run by a non-existent department. I was going to look into it when I had more…'

'Yes,' said the Doctor, 'I think you've had quite enough time for now, Andrew. But this is very good news, looks very likely this is our place.'

Amy took the piece of paper out of Andrew's hands and read it. 'But that address can't be right, Doctor.'

'And why's that?'

'Because,' said Amy, 'there is no self-storage at the Millennium Dome.'

'Shows what you know!'

They'd taken a cab over the Thames to the Millennium Dome. It was evening – Amy thought she must only have lived through this night once before, maybe twice, it was so hard to remember. They'd walked past the main entrance to the Dome, past the flashing lights and the huge awnings advertising the next big artists due to play gigs at the venue, round along a path that led them out by the river. It was quiet here, and the lights of the financial district skyscrapers were beautiful for being so distant and abstract. Each lit office was just an illuminated brick in the vast walls. Amy wondered what someone from another planet would make of a view like this – even she found it alien.

'What's that, Doctor?'

The Doctor pointed triumphantly to a small door half-concealed behind one of the many struts and sails of the Dome's structure. 'No self-storage at the Dome! What do you know?'

The door was very small. It wasn't even as tall as Andrew Brown, and he was the shortest of them. It looked like a piece of chipboard, badly painted with some khaki-green paint. There was no handle, just a cheap-looking brass lock. Next to the door was a buzzer, and above the buzzer was taped a piece of cardboard with the words 'Little Green Storage' written on it in black biro.

'I don't think this can be right, Doctor,' said Rory.

'It doesn't look like a half-a-million-pounds-a-month storage centre,' said Andrew.

The Doctor looked at them both and rolled his eyes.

He rang the buzzer.

They waited.

On the Thames, a couple of passenger boats cruised past. The river plashed softly. A car honked its horn somewhere back near the car parks.

Rory, Amy and Andrew looked at each other.

The Doctor looked at them. 'Well, I, er…'

The door opened, just a fraction. Inside was pitch-dark, it was impossible to see anything beyond the doorframe.

'Yes?' said a low voice like the creaking of an old hinge.

'Ah, hello,' said the Doctor, pulling out his psychic paper. 'I'm the Doctor, and these are my friends Rory, Amy and Andrew, and I was wondering if I could…'

'Ah yes,' croaked the voice, quietly. 'Doctor. How wonderful to see you again, and you're wearing a different body, I notice. How you do keep up with fashion. It suits you very well.'

'I, um, yeeees,' said the Doctor.

'Do come in. I imagine you'll be wanting to visit your storage locker. The contents are quite safe, I assure you.'

The door swung more widely open. The space beyond was still impenetrably black.

'Doctor…?' said Amy, in a warning tone.

'It's perfectly safe,' said the Doctor, ducking his head to go through the door, 'probably.'

Andrew glanced at the watch on his wrist, shrugged

and followed him. Rory and Amy looked at each other.

'After you,' said Amy.

Rory glared at her.

'I'm sure there's nothing to be frightened of,' said Amy.

'Then why don't you go… Oh, never mind. I don't see how they can store anything in there anyway, it can only be some backstage cupboards but…'

Rory stepped through the door.

Amy heard his voice as if it was coming from a great distance away saying, very faintly: 'Wow.'

She bent down and walked through the door. And on the other side was the world.

In Lexington Bank, a Symington had brought something into the storeroom where the TARDIS was parked. It was a glimmering thing, half concealed in the palm of his hand. Nadia couldn't quite see what it was until he placed it with surprising gentle grace on the TARDIS door.

It looked like a small glass half-sphere – about the size of a watch face, but bulging out in the middle. In the centre of it there was a tiny flickering motion, like a beating heart. And the beating was speeding up, faster and faster.

'I very much doubt any door can withstand the blast,' said a Symington.

'That amount of time concentrated in one place?' chuckled a Blenkinsop.

And Nadia knew exactly what the glass half-sphere was. A time bomb.

*

As Amy got her bearings back, she stopped feeling quite so dizzy. She managed to open her eyes for more than a fraction of a second and had to admit that it wasn't quite a whole world. But it was still pretty vast.

She was standing on a gantry, holding very tightly to the cold metal rail in front of her. The gantry led back to a small door, but it looked like the door was about half a mile away, and she didn't see how she could have got here from there in one step. But the more important problem, the thing she just couldn't get her mind away from was that the gantry was made of a metal grille, through which she could see straight down. And the drop went down for about two hundred floors.

Amy held on to the rail as if it was the only friend she'd ever had. She tried to breathe deeply. Her knees felt like water. She didn't understand. She wasn't usually afraid of heights.

A quiet croaking voice from behind her said: 'Ah yes, Doctor, I'm afraid the spatial shift does take some humans that way. You should have warned me that your companions were, ahem, delicate.'

'I'm. Not. Delicate,' muttered Amy through gritted teeth. 'I just don't want to look down, that's all.'

She felt Rory's warm hand close around her cold white knuckles.

'You can do it,' he whispered.

And she found that this infuriated her more than anything else. She shifted her hand away from Rory's, set her jaw, made sure her other hand was holding the rail extra tightly, and forced herself to open her eyes and look around properly.

'Wow,' she said.

Her head was still swimming, her knees were still more fluid than she usually liked them, she still thought she might buckle to the floor at any moment, but if she kept concentrating on how very solid the rail was under her hand she could look at the view.

They were suspended on the gantry in the middle of a vast circular bowl dug into the ground. It was the same shape as the Millennium Dome, like the exact mirror reflection of the Dome, dug into the ground. But bigger – much, much bigger. It looked like this space was about a hundred times larger than the volume of the Dome. And down as far as she could see the bowl was lined with lit walkways and numbered compartments.

'As you can see,' creaked the voice close to her left ear now, 'our facility is quite extensive. Well, ahem, it is extensive and we are quite reduced.'

She risked turning her head to look at the creature producing the voice. She didn't know what she'd expected. Some kind of toad maybe, from the croaking voice, or a sixty-a-day smoker. Instead, it was a small floating humanoid figure, about half a metre tall, wearing a black cowled robe and boots. It had a face a bit like a child's – big eyes and a button nose – but very white skin, almost pale blue. It was absolutely genderless – Amy had no way of working out whether it was male or female, and given the number of species she'd met which had only one gender, or three or, in one very complicated case, seventy-two separate genders, there was no reason she expected to tell. And it was carrying a cane with a blue ball on the end, although what it needed a cane for when it could clearly fly wasn't immediately clear.

'Welcome to Little Green Storage – the name is just our joke, you see – your repository for all your unnecessary accoutrements during your holiday on Planet Earth, the most frequently attacked, colonised, exploited and enslaved planet in the five galaxies! Better watch out!'

'The, ah, the Yomalet-Ram, did I pronounce that right, terrible with names,' began the Doctor – the Yomalet-Ram nodded politely – 'was just telling us how this facility works. Fascinating. See that up there?' He pointed up to the ceiling, an interlocking web of fine threads which looked like the bottom of a huge trampoline slung across the space. 'Up there is the Millennium Dome, suspended using several million superconducting filaments. Clever, eh?'

'That's the Millennium Dome?' said Amy. 'But the Dome's not that big, that must be five miles across! More!' She started to feel dizzy and sick – she'd thought looking down was bad but looking up was somehow even worse.

'Ah, well, you see, ah. That's the clever part, that's the part the Yomalet-Ram was alluding to, weren't you, Yomalet-Ram, when you said that we were quite reduced. We're under the Millennium Dome, but when we came through that door –' he pointed way back along the gantry to the door at the far end – 'we were shrunk! Down to about, what did you say?'

'Seven point five per cent of your original size,' said the Yomalet-Ram, pleasantly. 'We've found, over various planets and life forms, that any more compression can lead to permanent tissue damage.'

'Clever, very clever. That's why you've got a touch of

vertigo, Amy – your brain's having to calibrate a whole new set of spatial parameters. And it's only 7.5 per cent of its original size! Isn't that amazing!'

Amy rather wished the Doctor hadn't told her any of that. She realised that she'd half known it instinctively since she came through the door – that's why looking up was even worse than looking down – something felt very wrong. She stared very firmly at the rail that she was holding and her hands on it. She noticed a small cockroach crawling along the gantry by her foot. Strangely, this made her feel calmer – just the familiarity of seeing a normal, good old Earth cockroach felt like something safe to cling to.

'Can I go now, Doctor?'

The Doctor frowned. 'I think that's probably not a good idea. Stick together, we won't have to be here for long. Yomalet-Ram, I don't suppose you've got any anti-nausea pills Amy could take, something to ease the discomfort?'

The Doctor reached out to touch the Yomalet-Ram's coat. There was something odd about the gesture, but Amy couldn't work out what it was.

The Yomalet-Ram shook its head sadly and moved out of the Doctor's reach. 'We find that the worst of the symptoms pass away after a few minutes,' it said. 'Perhaps if you'd care to inspect the contents of your own storage container, the young lady might find the view a little less intimidating?'

The Doctor nodded. 'Good idea, good idea indeed. Take us to my storage container.'

The Yomalet-Ram smiled thinly. It was not a comforting smile or one with a great deal of warmth behind it. 'I'm sure you remember the protocol, Doctor.'

'Oh, ah, yes, the protocol, of course the protocol, yes silly of me, sorry. Just remind me?'

'I cannot accompany you to your storage container, Doctor. You must input your unique identification number onto the pad.' The Yomalet-Ram pointed its cane towards a numbered keypad welded to the rail, which Amy wasn't at all sure had been there until it pointed to it. 'The system will do the rest. Provided, of course, aheheheh, that you have the right palm print. As I'm sure you do.'

'Oh yes, all comes back to me now, silly thing – change of bodies, rattles the memories. Lose my own head if it weren't screwed on.'

The Yomalet-Ram smiled even more disconcertingly, if that was possible, made a tapping gesture with its cane and vanished. They were alone on the gantry.

'Do you… know that alien?' said Rory.

The Doctor shook his head. 'Not yet, definitely not yet, probably will sometime in the future. Hmmm… If I had to choose a unique code then there's really only one number I would have chosen…'

His hand hovered over the numbered keypad, which, when Amy looked, contained about twenty different digits only some of which she recognised.

'I wonder if I should just see if I've left anything for me. It's just the kind of thing I might do.' He frowned. 'But then, of course, it might not have been me at all. Lots of people going around the universe pretending to be me. Or I might have left a practical joke for me, that's just the kind of thing I might be going to be the sort of person to do, too…'

He chewed his upper lip thoughtfully, staring at the keypad.

'Doctor,' said Rory at last. 'Shouldn't we, you know, go and find the Lexington Bank storage locker? The one they're paying £454,909 a month for?'

'Mmmm?' said the Doctor.

'You remember, Doctor, that's why we're here?'

'What? Oh yes, good idea. Andrew, have you got that invoice?'

Andrew Brown – who, Amy was irritated to notice, wasn't suffering any ill effects at all from the miniaturisation process – pulled the paper from his pocket and unfolded it. Along the top, under the name of the Bank, was a long string of numbers and symbols.

'Very good!' said the Doctor. 'Well remembered! OK, let's just type in the number and—'

'Wait, Doctor,' said Rory. 'How are we going to get into the locker? They said we'd need a palm print?'

'Quite right, Rory, we'll need a palmprint, and that would be a terrible problem if –' the Doctor fished around in his jacket and produced a slim silver object like a long thin fish that wiggled slightly when he touched it with his index finger – 'if I hadn't picked the Yomalet-Ram's pocket for the master key when he wasn't looking. Come on!'

He turned back to the keyboard and punched in the number.

Chapter 12

There was a horrible whooshing sensation. Amy noticed the feeling – and how nauseatingly awful it was – before she realised what was happening, which was that the gantry they were standing on was falling, very fast, towards the centre of the basin.

She tried not to scream but didn't quite manage it.

The Doctor was holding on to the rail, the wind blowing through his hair, grinning. 'Nothing to worry about!' he shouted. 'Perfectly safe! Controlled freefall with inertial compensators, look!'

He pointed behind them. And she saw that the gantry hadn't actually broken off, leaving them falling into the miles of empty air. They were still attached to the outer edge of the basin, it was just that they were being swept down past the two hundred storeys of stacked storage containers, each with its own individual door. They started to slow as she watched. The flat bottom of the basin was still rushing towards them but it felt less like a terrifying fall and more like a ride now she knew they were safe. The gantry lurched suddenly to the side and zoomed them around the outside of the basin.

It stopped abruptly, facing a bank of forty or fifty doors. Above the whole bank of doors was the long number from the invoice. On each door was a metal plate with a space for a hand print, as well as several spaces for tentacle, pseudopod, leaf, paw and various unidentifiable appendage-prints.

'But which one is it?' said Andrew.

'Perhaps you're just supposed to know which one's yours,' said Rory. 'Like added security?'

'Right!' said the Doctor. 'Shall we take a look in a few?'

'Can we do that, Doctor?' said Rory. 'I mean, isn't it a bit… immoral? Looking at people's stuff?'

'Oh, I don't know, Rory, you'd be surprised what useful, not to say universe-saving things you can find out by taking a quick rummage through people's possessions. Don't worry, we'll put everything back where we found it.' He pulled the little silver fish-key out of his pocket and walked over to the first door. 'Better let me go first. You never know, there might be some kind of defence system.'

Ignoring the handprint space, he placed the master key close to the door. It wriggled and flowed outward, filling one of the handprints with its silvery liquid self.

The door clicked and unlocked. As the Doctor began to gingerly open it, a flurry of snow blew outwards and landed at his feet. Amy saw another cockroach scuttling through the snow.

'Hmm,' said the Doctor. He poked his head round the door. A snowball came sailing above his head and crashed into the gantry's safety rail. There was a sound of hoof beats and a hunting horn. He hurriedly closed the door and peeled the key off the lock.

'Definitely not that one,' he said, striding over to the next door.

'Was that...?' began Rory.

'No, Rory. That was absolutely not Narnia. Where do you get these ridiculous ideas from? Next!'

Nadia tried pulling the glass bomb off the door, but it wouldn't budge. And every time she came close to it, it set some weird mechanism off in her own watch – she could feel herself starting to age again as she grappled with it.

There had to be another way, though. She looked at the faces of the Symingtons and Blenkinsops – their rapt, worshipful expressions. She'd seen bankers look like that when they contemplated an enormous trade. What was in this box that they wanted so much?

'There's a displacement system,' said a Symington.

'No matter,' said a Blenkinsop. 'Our device will radiate back in time. It won't escape.'

Nadia knew, with complete conviction, that it would be a bad idea for the Symingtons and Blenkinsops to get their hands on anything they wanted so much.

The slow ticking sped up. There must be something that she could do. And then she realised.

There were a lot of doors. Amy rapidly began to lose count of how many they'd checked, although she knew she'd never be able to forget some of the contents. There was the room apparently filled with soap bubbles, and another completely full of string-like yellow roots, as if of a vast tree somewhere else entirely. One, when the Doctor opened the door gingerly, blew wide open. The storage container was totally empty but there was a huge gale coming from it, without any apparent source at all. The wind was so strong that it knocked Andrew clean over, and it took all four of them to slam the door closed again.

After a few doors, the Doctor became more cavalier and let them try some. Amy got a room full of mirrors which reflected her back to herself with differences which were at first subtle and then, as she looked, became more and more obvious. There was a reflection in which she was older, with a wise and kind expression, as if she knew a thing or two. There was one where she was scarred and dirty and far too thin. There was one where she was fighting off monsters – they were just off the edge of the mirror, she only saw the odd spider-like leg come into view – like a superhero. And another where she was tinkering with a piece of machinery that she knew instantly was alien technology – she was expertly wielding a white-beamed sonic screwdriver with five split beams. Amy took a step towards her reflections.

'Best not look too long,' the Doctor closed the door in front of her. 'Enough to enjoy in this dimension without getting confused by all the others. And just think,' he said, 'to some of those people, Leadworth would look incredibly exotic!'

Amy stood and stared at that door for a bit, while Andrew found a room staging live re-runs of *I Love Lucy*, and Rory got one made of mucus.

Mostly, though, the rooms were full of alien technology. There were ray guns and missiles, there were drifts of what the Doctor told them were computers the size of Amy's thumbnail, and transmat stations and purple-striped telepathy hats. 'Definitely not cool,' said the Doctor.

They found quite a few spaceships. 'Makes sense,' said the Doctor, 'parking in London's a nightmare. And have you seen the fines they give?'

One room looked disturbingly familiar. In the centre, there was a six-sided console, half finished with wires coming out of it and some parts completely missing. A glass time-rotor in the middle of the console looked wrong somehow – lop-sided and fuzzy. Several red-metal robot men were working on the console with soldering irons and yellow laser cutters, some of them consulting a book which looked as if it had been burned and retrieved, half-charred, from a fire.

When the door opened, the robots turned to look at the Doctor with what Rory could have sworn was a guilty expression.

'Yes,' said the Doctor. 'Don't think I can't see what you're up to.' He closed the door and muttered, 'Note to self: must come back and destroy that later.'

And then there was the room with all the shelves. The Doctor opened the door. The huge room beyond extended back about fifty metres and was about ten metres tall. Floor to ceiling, it was lined with shelves. And on each shelf was a green glass box, about the size of a house brick. Each brick was labelled, and inside each one there was the faintest trace of movement.

'Well,' said the Doctor, 'I think we've found it.'

*

Amy followed the Doctor into the storage unit. It was quite beautiful. The rows of green glass bricks shimmered with a faint internal light – it was like standing inside a cabinet made of ice with fading sunlight tricking in from the outside. In the centre of the room was something that looked a bit like a dentist's chair with a restraint around the waist and a monitoring screen next to the head. The Doctor touched the screen.

'Nasty,' he said. 'Time Harvesting chair, very hard to get out of, you never have any time to make your escape.'

He ducked his head down to look under the seat, blinked a couple of times in a puzzled way.

'Interesting,' he said. 'Interesting.'

Amy ran her fingertips along a row of bricks.

'Be careful with those,' said the Doctor, standing up. 'Each one of them's a person.'

Amy looked more closely at the glass boxes. The label on the front of each one was someone's name. She glanced at a few: 'Ismael Habibi', 'Dr P. McCormick', 'Emma Taylor', 'Alexandra Li', 'Philip Doyley', 'Benny Har-Even', 'Sydney Jane'.

'But there are thousands here, Doctor,' she said. 'Hundreds of thousands. More people than work in the Bank, definitely.'

'I think it's spread out from the Bank,' said Rory, pointing to one of the glass blocks.

Amy looked over his shoulder. 'But that's… isn't she in the Cabinet?'

Rory nodded.

'Look over here,' said Amy. 'He was on *X-Factor*, wasn't he?'

All around the room the little bricks shimmered, each one with its faint, almost indistinguishable tiny movement at the centre, like a transparent creature's minute heartbeat.

'So these are… the stores?' asked Amy. 'This is where they're keeping the time they've taken from everyone? They transfer it here from the watches, like, wirelessly? Like the internet? So if we broke all these blocks, everyone would get their time back?'

'Hmm,' said the Doctor. 'Hmm.'

'What?' asked Rory.

The Doctor closed his eyes and stretched out his arms to the side. His fingers were moving as if he were touching the glass bricks, but he wasn't near them. He went very quiet and still. He murmured something under his breath. He snapped his eyes open.

'No,' he said. 'Makes no sense. The thing is, Rory, you see, the thing is, time is a very volatile substance. Very dangerous to store, very hard to use, very hard even to keep track of. I mean, how do you have the time to work out how much time someone has borrowed, do you see what I mean?'

Rory shook his head. The Doctor ignored him.

'And they're doing something a lot more difficult than just storing. You're rather lucky, Rory, that you've got someone here whose physiology makes him sensitive to ebbs and flows in time, don't know what you would have done without me.'

Amy rolled her eyes. She looked around for Andrew and saw that he was reading his way along the names on the glass blocks, examining the tiny movement deep inside them. She noticed a cockroach crawling along one of the rows of bricks. It was quite a big one, about as long as her thumb. Amazing, she thought, they get everywhere.

'So you see,' the Doctor was saying, 'if this room were filled with all the time that they've taken from everyone, I'd be able to feel it. These are more like… the accounts. Each one protected, sheltered by these containers from the flow of time so that they can keep accurate records. Villains, Rory, real villains always like to feel that they're doing things by the book. They want records of exactly how wrong they've been. I remember Al Capone telling me that once. Or was it Genghis Khan? But there's something else.' The Doctor waved his arms at the walls of green-blue-grey glass. 'This is all very… showy… even for time-storage standards. It's almost as if they want to… show them off? Or maybe even…' He spoke more quietly, asking the question to himself rather than anyone else, 'sell them on? But that trade's been dormant since the Time War, it's…'

'So these are just… everyone's bank statements?' interrupted Amy.

The Doctor spun on his heel, took a deep breath and said: 'Bit more complicated than that, bit more difficult to arrange when you're talking about time. But basically, yes.'

Amy shrugged, 'Isn't it the same then, Doctor? If we destroy them all, no one will owe anything any more. End of story.'

'Or if we destroy them all, everyone will instantly pay back whatever they owe right now.'

'Oh,' said Amy. 'Right.'

'Or nothing will happen, or they'll destroy the

universe. Hard to tell without knowing what's going on inside them.' He shrugged. 'But they're so pretty, aren't they… I wonder who they expect to see them…' He drifted off again.

Andrew Brown had been quiet for a long time. He was standing in front of one of the shelves of glass bricks, staring at one particular block, gazing at the tiny beating heart.

Rory went over to him, looked over his shoulder.

The brick Andrew was staring at was labelled with his own name: Andrew Brown, Lexington Bank.

Rory put his hand on Andrew's shoulder. 'Oh, mate,' he said. 'Oh, I'm sorry, that's—'

Andrew shrugged the arm off. 'I did it to myself,' he muttered softly. 'No one else to blame.' He reached out and picked up the brick, held it in his two hands. 'No one else to blame,' he said again.

Rory stood silently by his side, watching a really massive cockroach – about as long as his index finger – scuttle across the floor.

'So what should we do now, Doctor? If we're not going to just –' Amy motioned punching one of the glass bricks – 'smash them all?'

The Doctor bent over slightly to examine one of the blocks. The name on it was Lee Frakes, Wandsworth, London. Inside, there was the same light as all the others, the same faintly flickering movement.

'Doctor…' said Rory.

'Just a moment, Rory,' said the Doctor. 'Look at this, Amy, do you see that?'

Amy looked at what the Doctor was pointing at. There was a faint hairline crack all the way around the glass brick, near the top. Now that she was looking, Amy saw that all the bricks had a similar faint line around them.

'Is that… a lid?'

'Only one way to find out.' He reached out gingerly and tried to lift the lid off. It wouldn't come.

'Doctor…?' said Rory again.

'Not now, Rory,' said the Doctor. 'I'm trying a very delicate manoeuvre here…' He aimed his screwdriver at the crack. Nothing happened.

'Doctor,' said Rory. 'There's a… cockroach.'

'I've seen them, Rory,' said Amy. 'They're everywhere. Just don't fuss at it and nothing will…'

'I don't think… I don't think you've seen one like this…'

Amy heard a chitinous clicking from behind her. She'd never heard a cockroach click before. She turned her head very slowly.

Beside Rory was a cockroach.

It was about the size of a kitten, but several million times less cute.

And it was growing as she watched.

'Doctor…' she said. 'Doctor…'

'Hang on.' He was holding his sonic screwdriver in his teeth, aiming it at the glass box, while trying to lift the top part of it up.

The cockroach clicked its mouthparts. It waved its long antennae. They were as thick as a pencil now, about a metre long and, like the rest of it, growing.

'Doctor…' said Amy again.

'Hang on a minute, this thing just won't…'

'This is more important, Doctor!'

The Doctor looked up. He saw the cockroach.

'Ah,' he said, 'yes, I thought that might happen. Automatic defence system set up by the very wise and prudent Yomalet-Ram.'

'All very interesting, Doctor, but – cockroach!' shouted Amy, backing away. She thought of picking up one of the glass bricks and hurling it at the insect, but remembered what the Doctor had said about destroying the whole universe and thought better of it.

'Probably not actually just a cockroach?' said the Doctor, backing away too, keeping Amy, Rory and Andrew behind him as they slowly moved out of the storage unit. The cockroach was the size of a Labrador now, but a lot less friendly. 'You see how it's not damaging any of the stored items?' The cockroach was feeling its way towards them, brushing its antennae softly along the shelves. 'But it knows we're intruders. Genius! Probably at least genetically modified, maybe some kind of mind-control chip embedded in it, very clever. Do you see?' He stopped moving momentarily and turned round to face Amy. 'Actually the cockroach is just reverting to normal size, whereas we're still tiny, probably takes a lot less energy than actually creating an enormous cockroach. It's very clever.'

'Doctor!' Amy screamed, the cockroach was almost on him, its mandibles opening and closing, showing their serrated edges, its horrible little head-legs reaching for them.

'Right, yes,' said the Doctor, 'out!'

Chapter 13

They ran back out onto the gantry. Andrew had grabbed the block with his name on it as they left and clutched it to his chest. The cockroach was following them, dribbling a yellowish liquid.

'Oh, that's new,' said the Doctor. 'That must be some kind of modification. How fascinating. Just a moment.' He rooted around in his pockets, found a notebook, a gobstopper, a ball of string and finally a handkerchief. He rolled the handkerchief up and threw it at the giant cockroach. A little of the yellow fluid splashed onto the fabric and it dissolved with an acid hiss.

'Hmm,' said the Doctor. 'Clever!'

'Never mind about that, Doctor, let's just get out of here!' screamed Amy.

She started randomly punching numbers into the keypad. The gantry lurched first to the right, then up, then rapidly down again. The movement made the cockroach skitter from side to side. A few drops of its acid saliva dripped onto Rory's coat, which immediately started to hiss and blacken. He pulled it off and threw it to the floor where the yellow acid continued to eat away at it.

'Don't. Do. That. Again!' shouted Rory.

'All right! So what *do* we do?'

The Doctor examined the keypad frowning. 'There must be a way to make it go back up to the entrance, there must be a...'

The cockroach advanced slowly, but inexorably.

'Wait,' said Rory. 'We're all right! I know what to do!' He rummaged in the partially dissolved coat at his feet and pulled the fully intact Super Lucky Romance Camera from his pocket.

'We just need to trap it, and we're OK!' he shouted.

The cockroach was advancing on them. Amy noticed that there were another three or four tiny cockroaches on the gantry. They were just ordinary size, but she didn't trust them to stay that way. The giant cockroach moved closer. One of its antennae brushed her sleeve. She shuddered uncontrollably.

'Now!' she shouted.

Rory clicked the Super Lucky Romance Camera button. There was a whirring noise. A small bubble appeared around the cockroach. It probed the bubble with its antennae and the wobbling exterior popped with a faint sighing sound. Rory stared at the cockroach. He shook the camera. He tried again. Nothing happened at all. The screen on the back of the camera displayed a message: 'LOW POWER, PLEASE TO RECHARGE BATTERIES FOR MORE LUCKY ROMANCE MOMENTS.'

'Low battery!' shouted Rory at the camera. '*Low*

battery? You're supposed to be a fifty-first-century piece of technology! You're supposed to have a cosmic radiation battery that picks up the background energy of the universe!' He looked at Amy, panic rising in his voice. 'It's not supposed to be able to run out of battery!'

The cockroach was feeling for Amy with its antennae. She shuddered again, looked the thing in the face and shouted: 'I've stomped your cousins into mush!'

She dived forward and kicked the cockroach hard in the mouthparts. The sole of her boot hissed at the contact with the acid. The cockroach fell back off the gantry, but flipped in mid air and clung on to a doorway ten floors below them. It began to crawl back up towards them. And it wasn't alone. From the bottom of the basin, more cockroaches were coming. Some were smaller, some were bigger. There was one cockroach slowly lumbering up the side of the basin which was the size of a Mini.

'Doctor!' screamed Amy. 'They're coming!'

'Right, no choice!' shouted the Doctor. 'Come here. We're going to look in my storage locker!'

He pressed a series of numbers into the keypad far too quickly for Amy to see what they were. With a dreadful lurch, the gantry swung round, but instead of swooping up and away from the approaching giant cockroaches, it started to descend towards the centre.

Nadia had never even used her own watch that much – she felt pretty aggrieved about that. She knew for a fact that the Head of Human Resources had borrowed weeks at a time – once he'd done it to go skiing with his family the same week the legal department were downsized.

And since it had started going wrong she hadn't dared to borrow any more time. But, well, it was worth a try.

She ran back to Storeroom F. She didn't want to be around the Symingtons and Blenkinsops when she tried it – that really might make them notice her. She fixed her watch with a steely stare, willing it not to go on the fritz while she was trying this. It rewarded her with a tiny shower of sparks. Right.

She turned the dial back an hour. She looked around. Nothing had changed, but the clock on the wall read an hour earlier. She chuckled softly. It had worked. She looked around. Something heavy would come in handy, but there wasn't much in this storeroom. She noticed the telephone directories on the shelf on the far wall. She walked over and picked one up, riffling the pages, hefting it in her hand to feel the weight. Smiled. Yes, this would do. She walked back to the storeroom with the TARDIS in it.

She didn't notice the echo she left, rippling backwards in time from her broken watch.

They were lucky the gantry moved so quickly. Even with the scuttling pace of the roaches, they swung round too fast for the creatures to quite keep up. But, Amy realised, if they had to try another fifty doors they'd be sunk. There was no way that they'd be able to fend the cockroaches off for long enough. She could feel where the sole of her boot she'd kicked the first one with was now much thinner than the other – paper thin. They only had seven boots left between them. Not enough.

But when the gantry lurched to a halt, there was only one door. They all ran to it. It was large and black and had the words *'Don't Come In Here – Seriously'* painted on the front in white paint. There was a single handprint-shaped pad on the door where the lock should have been.

The gantry started to rock. Underneath it, they could see through the grille, the cockroaches were climbing up the supporting struts, waving their vast antennae and drooling their foul yellow liquid.

The Doctor was running his fingers along the paintwork on the front of the door. 'I wouldn't warn myself unless there was a good reason,' he muttered. 'But then since I knew I was going to be here why would I take a unit at all if I didn't want me to come in? Puzzling, very puzzling.'

'They're coming!' shouted Amy. The car-sized cockroach had crested the top of the gantry and was putting its hairy articulated legs very carefully down onto the platform across from them. It wasn't hurrying. It had all the time in the world.

The Doctor looked round. 'Hmmm,' he said. 'Yes, good point well made'. He pressed his hand into the palm-shaped space.

The door opened. There was darkness behind it. The cockroaches were swarming across the gantry now. Amy, Rory and Andrew were trying to kick at them, but they were encroaching ever nearer nonetheless.

'Come on!' said the Doctor, walking into the darkness.

Rory and Andrew followed without hesitation. Amy, thinking of the vertigo she'd experienced on the roof, lingered for a moment. But only a moment. In a choice between vertigo and giant cockroaches, there was no comparison. She walked through the door, bracing herself for whatever weirdness lay beyond.

'Oh,' said Amy.

The four of them were crammed into a tiny vestibule the size of a small lift. There was another locked door in front of them, with another hand-recognition plate on the front of it. There was barely any room to move at all in the little cubicle. A groping antenna started feeling its way round the door they'd just come through. Amy slammed that door. The space got a little tighter. They were safe, but they couldn't stay here very long.

'Go on then, Doctor,' said Amy. 'Open the next door.'

The Doctor wormed his arm up from where it was pressed between him and Andrew and pressed the palm of his hand to the plate on the door.

Nothing happened

He stared at his hand, shook it vigorously and tried again.

A little window opened in the front of the door, with a message on a dot-matrix screen: 'I DON'T THINK YOU SHOULD COME IN HERE.'

The Doctor kept his hand pressed to the panel.

The message changed. 'YOU REALLY SHOULDN'T BE HERE YET AT ALL.'

The Doctor waited.

The message changed again. 'OH, ALL RIGHT. HAVE THESE. BUT REALLY, DON'T COME IN.'

A drawer pushed out from the middle of the door, hitting Rory in the solar plexus. Inside it were an enormous aerosol can, about as long as the Doctor's forearm, and what looked like a magazine article and a couple of batteries in a sealed freezer bag. The Doctor took them out and the drawer closed.

'Honestly,' said the Doctor, 'my other selves can be so patronising. Do this, go there, be careful not to destroy the whole of space and time.'

'But does that mean that some future version of you has been here?' said Rory.

'When you travel in time as much as I do,' said the Doctor, 'you learn not to ask questions of yourself. Only leads to trouble. Anyway, look what we have here!'

He thrust the magazine article and batteries in the bag into his jacket pocket and held up the aerosol can. It was labelled 'Super Zap Cockroach Spray. Made on Kotorsk-Bejal, the fun-loving planet where the roaches are three metres tall!' There was a picture of a man – wearing jeans and a T-shirt, perfectly normal-looking in every way apart from having seven arms – holding the spray up to a cockroach towering above him.

'A… bug spray?' said Amy, unconvinced.

'There are planets with… giant cockroaches?' said Rory, wondering whether the Doctor would have to visit one some time soon to pick up the spray.

'You're really an… alien?' said Andrew.

They all looked at him.

'I thought maybe you were joking,' he said, plaintively.

Nadia was there, this time, before the Symington put the bomb on the TARDIS door. She saw the wave of expectation again as he arrived, watched the glimmering thing in his hand as he reached for the door and –

WHAM! – hit him sharply on the back of the hand with her hefty telephone directory.

The bomb fell to the floor. The Symingtons and Blenkinsops pushed against each other, trying to grab it, but Nadia was quicker. As she picked it up, she felt the effect on her watch again, the pull tugging the time out of her. Was this what it was supposed to do to the TARDIS?

Her watch fizzed and hissed. The Symingtons and Blenkinsops looked towards her, puzzled. She wouldn't have a chance if they saw her now. And the bomb was ticking fast. It was pulling strangely towards her watch now – as if they were both magnetised. She stopped trying to pull them apart. Better whatever was going to happen should happen to her, not to the TARDIS. Anything to stop the Symingtons and Blenkinsops getting in.

She smashed the bomb onto her watch, just as the ticking grew so fast that it was just a line of noise, a white flash inside the device.

Nadia's watch blew sparks and showers of glass dust. She wondered, her mind wandering already, whether it was the watch's broken state which had saved her. Her hands wrinkled. Her back bowed. The Symingtons and Blenkinsops backed away nervously from the time machine which seemed to have more tricks up its sleeve than they could hope to understand.

And Nadia crawled out into the corridor. Her watch's face was flashing up random numbers. Some of it was hanging off by a few wires. But the thing still wouldn't come off. And she was still ageing.

Confused, and so old now, much older than she'd

ever been before, she crawled half-conscious back to her station outside the Bank by the warm air vents.

'How are we going to get out, though?' Rory whispered.

They could hear the cockroaches scuttling all over the door.

'If we try to get one, the rest of them will get us,' whispered Amy.

Andrew slowly rolled up his left sleeve. 'Give me the spray,' he said.

'No,' said Amy. 'Andrew, you can't. You already owe them so much, you…'

'Hey, on top of 55,000 years, what's another few years? Give me the spray.'

The Doctor passed it to him.

'Right,' said Andrew.

They watched him do it. Holding the spray, he opened the door and began spritzing the contents all around him with his left hand, while simultaneously turning back the watch with his right hand. Another Andrew appeared next to them, spray in hand, attacking the cockroaches in a different direction. And another, and another, each one yelling a battle cry and running through the cracked-open door spraying giant-insecticide as fast as they could.

After a few seconds, Amy, Rory and the Doctor saw that there was no yellow fluid trickling down the inside of the door and ventured out behind the Andrews. There were ten of them, spraying the insects, which were rolling over, choking, kicking their head-legs. They turned to Amy, grinning, pointing at her wrist. 'Want to join in?' one of them said, proffering a spray can at her.

Amy shook her head. 'No,' she said. 'I think I've borrowed enough already.' She couldn't meet Rory's eyes.

The Andrews shrugged. 'Suit yourself.' He went back to spraying the bugs with more glee than Amy had ever seen on his face.

When the last one was gone, the platform, as if on command, started to glide smoothly up the side of the upside-down Dome towards the exit level. The Yomalet-Ram was waiting for them, hovering in mid air, when they got there.

'Ah, Doctor,' it said, with all appearance of courtesy. 'I can't tell you how glad I am you survived. Of course, I knew you would. But you know how these things are. I have certain contractual obligations to protect the property in my care. I can't call off the roaches for just anyone. No matter how… aheheh… lucrative a client.'

The Doctor nodded. 'Time to go now.'

The Yomalet-Ram made a sweeping motion with his hand to indicate the exit door. 'The tissue decompressor will have stored your bio-imprint to a 99.99999 per cent accuracy. You may find the odd, aheh, hair on your head in the wrong place.'

Amy looked at the Doctor.

'Let's go,' said the Doctor.

'Oh, before you do,' said the Yomalet-Ram, 'do take my card. I know you'll have a use for it. In the past.'

The Yomalet-Ram smiled properly for the first time since they'd met it. Its teeth were small and pointed. Its smile was not a comforting thing.

The Doctor glanced at the card and thrust it into his pocket. 'I rather hope I find another way,' he said.

'Oh, I know,' said the Yomalet-Ram. 'But you won't.'

It was dawn when they left the Little Green Storage. Amy didn't quite know how that'd happened. She knew they'd been in there a while, but it had felt like a few hours, not a whole night. The Doctor muttered something about compression causing temporal distortions, what with matter being the same as energy, but it went over her head. She found a scrubby patch of grass to sit on. She'd rarely felt so glad to see daylight.

Rory came and sat down next to her. He took her left hand in his and rolled up the sleeve.

'I saw you had one of these,' he said, 'but I didn't think you'd... But you have, haven't you?'

Amy nodded.

Rory put his arm around her. She didn't resist. He rested his head on her shoulder.

'Oh, Amy,' he said. 'Why?'

She moved awkwardly. 'I wanted to be in two places at once,' she said. 'I wanted to try to make everyone happy. To be a daughter and a wife and a friend and... and me.'

'How much did you borrow?'

'It doesn't matter,' she said. 'Too much and not enough.'

A little distance away, the Doctor was leaning against the fence watching dawn break over the Thames.

Andrew stood next to him, the empty aerosol can of bug spray under one arm, the glass brick he'd taken from the store sticking out of his jacket pocket.

'Did we find out anything useful, Doctor?' said Andrew.

'In the storage container?' The Doctor shrugged. 'No, not particularly. We know where they're keeping the records, but we have no idea where the central time store is, or how to disable it. We don't even know who let them into the Bank in the first place.'

Andrew stared at the glass brick, the one with his name written on the front. 'Might there be an answer in here?'

The Doctor took it from his hand and looked at the hairline crack along the side. 'If I could get inside it to take a look at the mechanism, maybe.'

Andrew Brown looked at the glass box with his name on. 'I owe them 55,000 years?' he said.

The Doctor nodded.

'And lots of other people do too? And probably even more than I owe?'

The Doctor nodded again.

'And if we find out who's responsible and where they're storing the time, maybe we can get everyone's time back and none of this will have happened?'

'Maybe,' said the Doctor.

'And the information in here could help you find out?' said Andrew.

'Could be,' said the Doctor. 'No guarantees.'

Andrew Brown hefted the glass brick in his hand, as if trying to decide how much it weighed. Feeling the value of every borrowed hour, everything he'd signed away without really realising how much he was giving up. The weight of a life.

He raised his arm high. He was going to drop the block to the stone path, to shatter into tens of thousands of tiny gleaming shards.

'No!' shouted Rory, jumping up to grab his arm, wrestling the glass slab from him.

'It's the only way,' said Andrew. 'I made my own decisions, I have to take the consequences.'

'No,' said Rory, turning the brick over. 'Not yet. Look.'

On the base of the brick, embossed into the glass, in very tiny letters which looked darker green against the pale material, were the words 'PRIVATE PROPERTY. IF FOUND, RETURN TO THE OFFICE OF VANESSA LAING-RANDALL, LEXINGTON BANK.'

Chapter 14

'So we do have to go back to the Bank,' said Amy. She scratched at the watch on her left wrist. The skin around it was getting quite sore from all her worrying at it.

'Not you,' said Rory. 'We want to keep you well away from those Symingtons and Blenkinsops.'

'None of us can go there,' said the Doctor. 'They know us now. We won't be able to sneak around. Unless…'

'Unless?' said Amy hopefully.

'Hmmm,' said the Doctor. 'We need to find Nadia Montgomery again. I need to take another look at her watch. But Andrew, we need you.'

Andrew nodded. 'I need to tell the others what's going on.'

'Well, that,' said the Doctor. 'But also to find out what's going on in Vanessa Laing-Randall's office…'

Nadia drifted in time. Sometimes she was young again, so young that she felt well and strong. But those were only moments. There, and then gone. Sometimes she wondered if she simply imagined them. Perhaps the dream of being young was a delusion of being old. And her memory was so fragmented. She had no memory of growing old, but perhaps that was part of her madness too. She tried to figure it out herself, over and over, muttering her calculations, reminding herself that she was not, she was not, she was not crazy.

She never wandered far from the Bank, was never able to. But sometimes kind people helped her. Like the kind young man who took her by the arm and said, 'Nadia? Is that you? Nadia, Head of Marketing?'

She almost recognised him, just for a moment.

'Andrew?' she said, but then the memory faded.

He took her to Temple Gardens, where a green baize lawn led down almost to the Thames, as if someone had laid out a carpet. There were three nice young people waiting for her there with a thermos flask filled with hot chocolate and cheese sandwiches.

'That shoe needs resoling,' said Nadia to Amy.

She'd told them what she'd done – as best as she was able. They were grateful, if a bit confused. She couldn't tell it quite right, everything was muddled. Shoes, though, still made sense.

Amy looked at the underside of her boot where the sole was paper thin. 'Yeah well,' she said. 'We're all a bit the worse for wear, eh?'

The Doctor was fiddling with Nadia's watch. The thing let out sparks from time to time, and sometimes it vibrated so quickly that it seemed to almost vanish for a moment.

'What are you doing, Doctor?' asked Amy. 'I thought you already got my watch to mimic Nadia's?'

'Mimic it, yes, yes that's right,' muttered the Doctor, holding his sonic screwdriver in his mouth while he tried to insert the end of a paperclip into the crack in Nadia's watch. 'But what this watch does isn't the only important thing about it.'

Amy and Rory exchanged a look – the look that said, 'Yes, he may be a Time Lord, last of his kind, travelling the length of time and space and being pretty sexy with it, but I almost never understand what he's going on about and nor do you.'

'Aha!'

The watch spurted a thin stream of silver sparks, and then stopped.

'Hmm, maybe not.' The Doctor removed his screwdriver from his mouth. This made him at least ten per cent more comprehensible. 'The thing is, all those Symingtons and Blenkinsops are the same creature, right? At different points in its time stream.'

'Yup,' said Rory. He'd definitely understood that part. Probably.

'So the reason that they ignore Nadia's watch isn't just because it often makes her invisible to them. It's also that they know it belongs to her.'

'Huh?' said Amy.

'They ignore her because they know her watch is broken. If we can get the field of her watch to extend to cover us, they'll ignore us, too.'

Nadia's watch spurted out a puff of black gas. The Doctor waved it away, coughing. Nadia became rapidly younger, de-ageing by about ten years in a heartbeat, her wrinkles smoothing out, her hair becoming thicker, her back unbending.

'Hmm,' said the Doctor. 'I didn't mean to do that. Not quite there yet.'

Andrew walked towards Sameera's office. She was behind her desk, tapping away at what he was sure was yet another perfect presentation that would make his efforts look like a schoolboy's homework. And, out of the corner of his eye, he saw her again, at the far end of the corridor, carrying some paperwork. How had he not noticed long before that she was in several places at once? That lots of people in the Bank were? Perhaps because that's how they were all supposed to be. Everyone in the building was supposed to give the illusion that they could be in nine different places at the same time, that they could do fifty hours' work in five, that nothing was ever too much. Everyone was supposed to pretend that the Bank was the most important thing in their lives and they always gave a mathematically impossible 110 per cent. He'd thought he was the only one who was struggling. But now he looked he saw that half the people working on this floor had tell-tale bumps under their sleeves on the left-hand side.

'You missed the meeting,' Sameera said as he walked into her office.

'The… meeting?' It felt like a hundred years since he'd last been in this building. Or even fifty-five thousand.

'There was a meeting you were supposed to be at this afternoon. Don't worry, I covered for you.'

'How much time did you have to borrow to do that?' said Andrew.

Sameera looked at him, considering. Then she shrugged. 'Nothing I can't pay back.'

'Oh, really?' said Andrew. 'You think so? Let me tell you something about their accounting system.'

Nadia was 50 now, and crying. The Doctor just looked embarrassed. Rory fished a handful of paper napkins from the sandwich bag and gave them to her.

'It's always worst when I'm younger,' she sobbed into the tissues. 'When I'm old, I forget everything. I don't know there's anything to be upset about. But then, when I'm a bit younger, I remember.'

Amy patted her on the back and looked glumly at her own watch.

'I'm only 40,' Nadia wailed. 'I thought there was time for everything. Time to meet someone and settle down, maybe even have a family. And now look at me.'

'There could still be...' Amy couldn't even finish the sentence. Nadia was getting older again in front of her eyes.

The Doctor was still tinkering with Nadia's watch. At last, there was a fizz of orange sparks which surrounded them all – Amy and Rory and the Doctor too – and then slowly faded away to nothing. Nothing except that, when Rory looked at his arm side-on he could see a faint glow still surrounding him.

'There, got it!' said the Doctor. 'Of course, that does mean that... hmmm... and we'll need a...'

Nadia stared at him, tears wet on her cheeks.

'The Doctor will fix everything,' Amy said to Nadia. 'He always, always finds a way to fix it.'

Nadia shrugged. 'What's he going to do, change the past?'

'You'd be surprised,' said Amy.

'I just can't stop thinking of everything I've lost,' said Nadia. 'All the places I wanted to visit that I'll never see, all the things I wanted to do with my life... the children I'll never have...'

The Doctor turned his head sharply and looked at her. 'The children you'll never... Yes, that's very interesting. Very interesting indeed.'

Sameera sat back in her chair with a heavy thud.

'I did know,' she said, 'about the compound interest. I've tried to be careful.'

'You have been careful,' said Andrew. 'More than me, anyway.'

The Doctor had shown him the trick to making the watches show how much time you owed in total. The display of Sameera's account hung in the air, glowing orange.

'BORROWED TIME TOTAL SINCE LAST REPAYMENT: 5 DAYS, 5 HOURS. INTEREST TERMS: 5 MINUTES PER HOUR, PER HOUR. TOTAL TIME OWED: 35 YEARS.'

'It's not your fault,' said Andrew softly. He'd never thought he'd feel sorry for Sameera, or even imagined they'd have much in common. In this building, where getting ahead was all that mattered, she'd always seemed like the enemy.

'I tried always to pay it back after a few hours, I knew the interest would pile up otherwise,' Sameera said. 'It's just, with this big new deal on and...'

Andrew nodded. 'We did this to each other,' he said. 'All those meetings where I felt like you'd be one step ahead.'

'But I wasn't!' Sameera said. 'Sometimes I had to leave to go to the loo to borrow the time so I could come back looking prepared!'

'I did the same thing,' said Andrew.

Sameera nodded. 'All those presentations where I kept trying to be just a bit better than you. All those client meetings where I just had to pull one more thing out of the bag…' She sighed and stared out of her office window at the glass atrium sculpture. 'We did this to each other. And now we've got to fix it.'

Amy patted Nadia's hand helplessly. She was about 60 now, still getting older.

'I don't know how to stabilise her,' said the Doctor. 'The only way is to get that watch off her.'

'This could happen to me too, couldn't it, Doctor?'

'Oh I think that's very unlikely,' the Doctor said, without much conviction. He shrugged. 'To be honest, I rather think we have something else to worry about. Show me your camera again, Rory.'

Rory pulled the useless Super Lucky Romance Camera out of his pocket. All it would do now was present increasingly pleading messages on its digital screen: 'NEW CHARGING IS REQUIRED. NO MORE LUCKY ROMANCE MOMENTS UNTIL CHARGING. PLEASE TO RECHARGE!'

'It used to have infinite battery life, didn't it?'

'That's what they told me when I bought it,' said Rory.

The Doctor rooted around in his pockets. At last he found the bag that he'd left for himself in the storage unit. He held it up. It was a plastic bag with the magazine article and a couple of batteries inside. Across the top of the bag, underneath the zip-lock strip, were the words 'Time proof to a depth of 40,000 years.'

'It's a time-bag,' said the Doctor. 'Like a freezer bag, only more useful. Prevents the contents from being affected by the passage of time or – and this is crucial, pay attention – or by ripples in the space-time continuum.'

'Ripples in the…'

'If I put you in this bag, Rory, sealed it and then went into the past and killed your grandfather, as long as you were still in the bag you'd be OK. Of course, then you'd have to live the rest of your life in a plastic bag, but there are worse things. There's a planet near Ursa Minor where they all have to live inside the stomach of a giant spinefish. The smell alone… So, could be worse, Rory, think of the upside! Where was I?'

'A time-bag,' said Rory.

'Ah, yes, quite right. So this is a time-bag. While the article is in here, it's protected from other changes in time. When we take it out, it won't be any more.'

'And then what'll happen?'

'I don't… know. Interesting, isn't it? Go on, have a read.'

Rory looked at the article in the bag. It was a short news piece, ripped from a paper magazine dated to the year 5013. 'Do they still have paper magazines in the fifty-first century?' he asked, puzzled.

'Some people still like them,' said the Doctor. 'It's probably edible paper, rich in vitamins and flavoured with the saliva of whoever wrote it. There's a bit of a fashion for that for a while.'

Rory wrinkled his face in disgust.

'As if *Big Brother* is any more normal. Just read the article.'

Rory read.

It was an article about a prize being awarded to the inventor of 'cosmic radiation power'. Professor Henrietta Nwokolo had been honoured, the article said, for the amazing innovations made by her and her team at Aberdeen University. The writer was full of praise for the amazing new power source. The article went on to say that teams in Japan and Australia had also been working on similar devices, but their versions were slower, and experienced sudden battery depletion. Underneath the article was an advert for Rory's Super Lucky Romance Camera mentioning the Super Infinite Cosmic Battery.

'OK...' said Rory. 'What does this tell us?'

'No idea,' said the Doctor.

'And what's going to happen if we take it out of the bag?'

'I don't know. Let's try!'

The Doctor unfastened the zip-lock. There was a hiss, and a strange kind of movement on the page of the article, like the letters rearranging themselves as Rory watched. He pulled the article out and looked at it. It wasn't much different. A bit shorter. It still started the same way: 'Team working on Cosmic Radiation Power awarded Buffett Prize' – but now the inventor was different, a professor at Tokyo University. And the praise for the invention was more measured – the technology wasn't perfect, there were sudden battery depletions to contend with, but nonetheless it was a real step forward.

The Doctor tipped the batteries out of the bag into his hand. 'I think you'll find those will re-power your camera, Rory,' he said, 'but maybe not for long, so be careful when you use them.'

Rory nodded, and slipped the batteries into his pocket. He stared at the magazine. 'But why did the article change, Doctor? I don't get it.'

The Doctor stared at the page. 'I do,' he said.

'What does it mean?'

'It means,' he said, 'that the people who made the breakthrough in that camera's technology never existed. They were never born. Your planet is losing its future. Piece by piece, the people are going.'

Sameera and Andrew were knocking on doors. It wasn't hard to work out who was using the watches, when they asked themselves. Who had suddenly had a burst of productivity over the past few months? Who had got in earlier than everyone else, left after everyone had gone home, but still wasn't divorced? Who had they been absolutely sure they'd seen on the fifth floor and then, moments later, spotted walking out of the building?

Andrew went to talk to a woman, Dorotea Kemal, who worked on the Scandinavian desk. He knew he'd seen her in the office working late on the very same night that he'd passed her laughing and joking with friends in a restaurant when he'd gone for a walk round the block. Sameera decided to approach Dan Logovik – an Australian in-house editor in his mid thirties who'd recently started to produce a huge volume of extra work.

Sameera bumped into Dan as he was leaving his office.

'Sorry,' she said.

'Sorry for what?' said the Dan who was sitting at his desk. She spotted another one across the atrium, his burly frame bent forward, eagerly talking to a senior saleswoman. How had they all got so careless so quickly? And how had none of the people in charge spotted it and stopped them? It was as if the higher-ups didn't want to know. As long as they kept making money for the Bank, that was all anyone cared about.

'Dan,' she said, 'I have to talk to you, it's really important.'

Dan's phone rang. She noticed him instinctively reach for his watch, stop himself, pause.

'Sameera, great to see you, brilliant, but listen I've got to take this phone call. Could you wait outside for a moment?'

She stood outside and waited. If he borrowed another few minutes to get that phone call on the first ring, so what? After a little while Dan popped his head round the door – he had that look she recognised, flushed with a combination of pride and worry.

'They've asked me to work on GCXP Holdings! I'm moving into analysis!' he said. 'It's the break I've been waiting for. I'll really be able to show them what I can do!'

Sameera nodded. 'We really need to talk, though, Dan, it's really…'

He grinned. 'My wife's going to be so proud,' he said. 'I can't wait to tell her. Look, let's have a chat. Just wait a second, there's something I've been meaning to do and I really don't want to put it off any longer.'

Sameera thought he was going to phone his wife. She

watched through the office window as he crossed the room and sat down at the desk. It took her a moment to realise that he wasn't picking up the phone, he was moving a dial on his watch.

'No!' she shouted. She opened the door, burst into the room.

But it was too late.

Excited and proud, Dan had evidently decided to pay back all the time he owed.

He fell, quite peacefully, forward onto his desk, his face a mass of wrinkles and his body a light, frail husk.

Sameera checked for a pulse, but it was as if he'd been dead for twenty years.

Chapter 15

'We're going to have to take her with us, wherever we go,' whispered the Doctor. 'It's the only way, for now.'

'How far do you think they've spread, Doctor?' Amy whispered.

They were loitering by the entrance to Bart's Hospital, waiting for their moment.

'In space or in time?' whispered the Doctor. 'What about that one?' He pointed to an elderly man being wheeled in through the doors in a wheelchair.

'We can't steal it from under him, Doctor, can we? Anyway, what do you mean space or time?'

'The more time they gather,' he muttered, 'the more fluid they become in time. The further back they'll be able to go. Soon we won't even have had time to hear of them. What about her?'

A pregnant woman in a wheelchair seemed about to get out of it and walk into the hospital but then let out a loud groan of pain and sank back in and allowed herself to be pushed through the doors.

'No good. Couldn't we just use the TARDIS, to go back before that?'

'Not if the timeline's already been rewritten,' said the Doctor. 'The TARDIS won't keep travelling back to an altered point in time, safety features. What about this?'

A nurse wheeled a woman with a broken leg through the door; he waited while her boyfriend helped her hobble into the waiting taxi. He turned round, pushed the chair back through the automatic doors and left it parked by the wall.

'Perfect,' said Amy. 'Come on.'

They marched towards the chair, both reaching for the handles at the same moment.

'I thought you were going to be the patient,' said Amy tetchily, trying to push the Doctor away from the handles.

'Have you never *heard my name*, Pond? I am never the patient, I am always the Doctor,' said the Doctor.

Their scuffle made some of the people waiting patiently in A&E look over at them.

'Doctor, just sit in the chair and let's *go*. There's clearly nothing wrong with me.'

'There's clearly nothing wrong with *me*.'

'Is there a problem here?'

A security guard had walked over very casually. Amy and the Doctor were both quite tall, but this man was taller still and quite a lot broader than either of them. He looked like he had balls of muscle in unexpected places like the tops of his shoulders and the backs of his arms.

'No problem,' said the Doctor. 'I'm the Doctor and my patient here—'

Amy reached into the Doctor's jacket pocket and

pulled out the psychic paper. She flashed it in front of the security guard. 'I'm Dr Pond,' she said, 'and this man is my patient.'

'No,' said the Doctor, 'I'm the Doctor and—'

'I'm afraid this man is a danger to himself,' Amy said. 'He's suffering from a delusion that he's a Doctor. I just need to get him into this wheelchair and take him to my… clinic.'

The security guard looked between them and then at the ID badge 'Dr Pond' was holding in her hand. His eyes locked on to it – that, he seemed to be thinking, was at least comforting, familiar, certain.

'What I don't understand,' said Rory, undoing the buckles, 'is why they tied him down.'

'It was for his own protection, wasn't it, Doctor?' said Amy, removing the blankets swaddling the Doctor's legs. He was seated in a very comfortable wheelchair. One of the ones with special Velcro restraints on the arms and legs and a nice tight seatbelt over his middle.

The Doctor glared at her. 'I could have got away. I didn't have to let them do it. I chose to because I, you see, am the bigger man.'

'Whatever you say, Doctor,' said Amy, helping him out and helping Nadia sit down on the comfortable padded seat. 'Whatever you say.'

Sameera and Andrew watched while the medical technicians prepared to take Dan's body away.

'How many people do you think have died here in the past six months?' Sameera asked.

Andrew stretched awkwardly. 'Let's see, there was

Brian Edelman, and Sara Hu, and that woman Linda from human resources and—'

'Do you remember Nadia Montgomery? Used to be Head of Marketing? Just disappeared one day?'

'Hmm, yeah, if you count all the people who disappeared…'

They stood in silence for a while as the people from the hospital loaded the sad frail body onto the wheeled stretcher.

'Maybe nine or ten? In the past six months?' Andrew said at last.

'That's quite a lot, isn't it? Even for an office this size, it's quite a lot.'

Andrew nodded.

The struts of the wheeled stretcher clicked into place. They stood aside as the body in its bag was rolled out of the room.

'Even one person dying in the office should have made us think about what we were doing,' said Sameera.

'We never thought about it in the years before all this, like all those times someone had a heart attack, do you remember? Remember Bob Leith?'

'Those weren't heart attacks, they were heart events.'

'He had four, though. All at the office. Before his wife made him retire.'

Across the atrium, the lift dinged. They were taking Dan away.

'We have to find out what's going on,' said Sameera. 'Before this happens to anyone else.'

Pushing Nadia in her wheelchair, it was easy to sneak in the back entrance of the Bank. They settled down in an empty meeting room, planned to wait there until Andrew and Sameera reported back.

Rory switched on the television to watch the news. No reports of aliens, of course. No sudden mass deaths or sudden rapid ageing all across London, that was good. But there was something…

'Doctor,' he said, 'look at that newsreader's arm.'

He was right: there, under the jacket of the man reading the news, was the tell-tale bump.

They watched the rest of the news in a sort of dazed horror. The watches weren't just in the UK. They saw one on the wrist of the mayor of a South American town, who was talking about how he managed to stay one step ahead of violent gangs. A surgeon in Oregon describing her invention of a life-saving new procedure which had to be administered within minutes of injury was wearing one. A team of scientists in Iceland who'd made a breakthrough in geothermal energy all had them on, not even covered by a sleeve.

'It's all good news, though, Doctor,' said Rory. 'Look at everything that's been done.'

'Yes,' said the Doctor. 'You can do a lot of brilliant things with extra time. You can do a lot of brilliant things with a fourth arm, too – doesn't mean it's a good idea to grow one, even if you are on a planet where it's all the rage. I should have remembered that, very hard to get your suits re-tailored for a fourth arm… Where was I?'

'But if we—'

'Rory. That's the trouble with borrowing. It makes everything look good. No one wants to see what's going on underneath because the surface is just so shiny. But there's no point –' he rounded on Rory, his eyebrows raised, his arms flailing – 'there's no point making everything shiny, if your whole species is going to die out the moment they call in those debts, is there?'

Amy nodded slowly. 'We have to find a way to warn them,' she said. 'And I think I know when we'll have the perfect opportunity.'

A Symington and Blenkinsop pair was walking along the corridor. Andrew and Sameera watched them from behind the potted plants on the tenth floor. They marched, in perfect unison, at an even, steady pace, like the ticking of a watch.

'Why did we never think of seeing where they went before?' asked Sameera.

'We were too busy competing with each other,' said Andrew. 'Didn't have any attention for anything else. I bet if aliens had announced they were going to blow up the planet, we would just have carried on working.'

Sameera grinned. 'We'd have issued competing memos on it.'

'Both of us trying to make a more complete analysis of alien life than the other,' said Andrew, smiling.

'In the hope that one of the aliens would promote us!' said Sameera.

Andrew laughed and then shushed himself.

Symington and Blenkinsop knocked in unison on the door of Vanessa Laing-Randall, head of the London office. They didn't wait for a response but walked straight in.

Sameera and Andrew waited for a long time to see if they'd come out again.

'What's happened to them?' hissed Sameera at last.

'Long meeting?'

'They never take that long selling anything to anyone. What do you think they're doing in there?'

'Well, if Laing-Randall's really their boss…'

'She did arrive at the same time that all this weird stuff started happening.'

'You mean, our amazing 300 per cent increase in productivity?'

'Yeah,' said Sameera. 'You know who'd know?'

'Who's that?'

'Come on,' said Sameera, leaving the cover of the pot plants and walking towards Vanessa's office.

Jane Blythe sat behind the most efficiently organised desk Sameera had ever seen. The pens were perfectly lined up on a side return, with a mosaic of sticky notes in different colours in tessellated order. There was a wall calendar behind her on which each event had been typed on a label-maker. The pins on the pinboard were arranged by colour. Nonetheless, Jane Blythe was distraught.

'I'm so glad someone's finally asked me about those weird men,' she said, on the verge of tears. Her shoulders shook in her business suit jacket and the pearls around her neck trembled.

'They come in here, they go into Vanessa's office –' she pointed to the door at the far end of her own office – 'and they never come out! I don't understand it. And then they come in again, and again, and again.'

Sameera and Andrew nodded sympathetically. It hadn't taken much to get Jane to talk to them; it was as if she'd been waiting for someone to share her fears with.

'Have you ever seen what they do in there?' asked Andrew.

Jane shook her head. 'I'm under strict orders from Vanessa never to go into the office when she's not there... She's very serious about it. I've never had a boss like her before. All the other executives I've worked for liked it when I rearranged their offices, you know –' she motioned to her obsessive-compulsive stationery arrangement – 'neatly. And answered their letters, and dealt with their appointment diaries...'

'There's something in there she doesn't want you to see, obviously,' said Sameera. 'We're going to take a look.'

The door wasn't locked, that was the odd thing. Vanessa Laing-Randall had obviously thought that her strict instructions to her assistant were enough to keep her out. And there was no one in the office at all.

'Where did they go?' asked Sameera.

Jane Blythe, hovering nervously at the door, said, 'I never know. They never come out.'

'Maybe,' Andrew muttered to Sameera, too low for Jane to be able to hear, 'they travel back in time instead. That's why we didn't see them. They left before we arrived.'

Andrew and Sameera checked through Vanessa's filing cabinet and laptop quickly. There wasn't anything obvious, no files labelled 'Top Secret Evil Alien Plans' or even 'What I Plan To Do With Everyone's Time Once I've Collected All Of It'. There was a locked door at the far side of her office, though.

'What's through here?' asked Sameera.

Jane was standing just over the threshold, clearly

terrified to be in the room without permission. 'I, um, I... I'm not allowed in there.'

'Come on, Jane, surely you know where she keeps the key? PAs know more than their bosses, we all know that,' said Andrew.

Jane hunched her shoulders with anxiety. 'Did you... I mean... um, have you spoken to anyone else about this?'

'A few of us have talked about it,' said Andrew, hunting through Vanessa's desk drawers for a key.

'And do any of you know what's going on?' Jane's voice was high-pitched with nerves.

'There's this one guy,' said Andrew distractedly, trying to peer behind a cabinet. 'The Doctor? He seems to know most about it all. Keeps going on about aliens, if you can believe it.'

Jane giggled nervously. She obviously didn't believe it at all. Then she said, 'Oh,' very quietly. And then again, louder. 'Oh.' With a jangle of terror in her voice.

Andrew and Sameera looked up.

Standing behind her were a Symington and Blenkinsop.

'Oh dear,' said Mr Symington.

'Well said,' said Mr Blenkinsop.

'I do believe that these young people...'

'So young, so naive, so full of promise.'

'Indeed, Mr Blenkinsop, indeed, I do believe that these naive young people are attempting to steal private property.'

'To gain access without permission.'

'A serious crime.'

'And as they well know,' said Mr Symington,

'committing any such crime will cause the immediate withdrawal of all loaned time.'

'What a terrible, terrible shame,' said Mr Blenkinsop, opening his shark mouth very wide.

Chapter 16

Jane Blythe acted more quickly than Sameera or Andrew would have believed possible. Seeing the hideous transforming faces of Symington and Blenkinsop behind her, she jumped forward into Vanessa Laing-Randall's office and slammed the door hard behind her. She locked it and turned round, staring wildly at Sameera and Andrew.

'Oh,' she said. 'Oh.' Her eyes rolled back, and she crumpled to the floor.

Something crashed into the door. Symington and Blenkinsop were trying to get in. They were charging into the door, banging into it, trying again and again and again.

Sameera patted Jane's face gently. Jane's eyelids flickered.

'Are you all right?' asked Sameera.

Jane opened her eyes slowly. 'Those really are… aliens, aren't they?' she said.

Sameera nodded.

'Before I fainted, I thought they were turning into sharks. Were they turning into sharks?'

Sameera shrugged. 'Maybe not actual sharks? Maybe just that they look a bit like sharks? I guess nature finds the same useful patterns in a lot of different places.' She paused. '*Aliens,*' she said to herself.

'And... Vanessa has something to do with them?'

'We think she's their boss,' said Andrew.

Jane blinked very rapidly.

'I know it's a shock,' said Sameera quietly, 'but we have to find some way out of here. They're going to get in eventually.'

'No.' Jane shook her head slowly. 'It makes sense. Ever since Vanessa took over running the London office, these terrible things have started happening. Like... have you noticed how sometimes you see the same person in two places at the same time?' She laughed slightly hysterically. 'I thought I was going mad.'

'We've seen it, too,' said Sameera. 'Everyone's seen it, they've just been ignoring it because it was easier than trying to work out what's going on.'

'You know...' said Jane, slowly, 'Vanessa always keeps the key to that door...' She nodded towards the door at the back of the room. 'She always keeps that door locked, always has the key with her. But once I saw it open – I wasn't supposed to be here, I was working late. And it was full of... I think it was full of green glass bricks? Isn't that weird?'

Sameera and Andrew exchanged a look.

'Not weird at all,' said Sameera. 'Not even a tiny bit weird. We need to let Amy and her friends know, though.'

'I've called Amy and the Doctor,' said Andrew. 'They're on their way. They might get here in time to help us.'

'The doctor?' said Jane weakly. 'Do I need a doctor?'

'No, he's... Well...' Andrew looked at Sameera. 'Yeah, we think he's an alien as well, to be honest. He seems to know a lot about time travel.'

'Amy said they travel in time with him,' said Sameera.

'Yeah, they seemed to know everything about what's going on here. Talked about "Time Harvesters"...'

Jane's eyes opened very wide.

The banging at the door halted for a few seconds. They stared suspiciously at the door, wondering if the Symington and Blenkinsop had given up. But then it resumed. There was longer between each bang but the sounds were louder. They were taking run-ups.

'Why do you think they haven't just come back in time to get here before us?' Andrew murmured, eyeing the door.

Jane said, 'I heard Vanessa say to one of them once that the office was... shielded? Is that the word? Because of the storage dangers?'

Sameera nodded. 'That makes sense. Still, they'll get in here soon enough.'

Jane looked at them both. 'You trust him, this Doctor? You trust him with your life?'

Andrew looked at Sameera. She had a funny half-smile on her face. He'd seen it on her in meetings when she knew she had the winning argument and was just waiting for her moment to use it. He hadn't realised how well he knew her face until just then.

'Well,' said Sameera, 'I trust him a hell of a lot more than I trust most of the people who work in this bank.'

'Can he save us?' said Jane. 'The Bank? Or the world? If you get to him and tell him what you know about Vanessa, will he be able to save us?'

Andrew opened his mouth and closed it again. In his work at the Bank, his job had always been to talk everything up, to say that things were going to be better than they really were. But he was never going to do that again.

'I don't know,' he said at last, 'but I don't think anyone else can do it.'

'You're going to bring him here?' Jane asked.

'He's on his way,' said Sameera.

'OK then,' said Jane.

Above her head, there were two almighty bangs as Symington and Blenkinsop took another run-up. The wood around the lock was starting to splinter.

'We don't have much time,' she said, 'but I know what to do.'

Nadia's watch was sparking purple and green. She stared at it. She was getting younger now, younger by the minute, by the second, she could feel it. It had happened so many times before, but each time, in each direction, it felt sickeningly wrong.

Rory was pulling her wheelchair into the goods lift at Lexington Bank. A wheel had stuck, she was bumping in her seat. The motion was doing something to the watch, something in it was jogging loose she could feel it and with it...

'Doctor!' she said, and her voice was higher than she'd expected, and lighter. 'Doctor, something's happening!'

'Right,' said the Doctor. 'Let's see if we can do something about that.'

He tinkered with her watch again with his little pen-like laser device. He rattled her wrist, then gave it one extra burst. She felt another lurch begin in her cells.

'Good,' he said. 'That ought to... Hmmm. That wasn't supposed to happen.'

'Doctor, she's—' began Rory.

'Yes,' said the Doctor. 'I can see that.'

'What's happened?' said Nadia, and her voice was so high-pitched and childlike that it startled her.

'You're um...' began Amy, wrinkling her brow, 'I don't know how to tell you this but you're, um...'

'You're about 10,' said the Doctor. 'We'll have to fix it, but not right now. Come on, at least we can leave the wheelchair.'

They set off at a sprint up the stairs. And Nadia, more full of energy at least than she'd been for years, began to run with them.

In the outer office, Symington and Blenkinsop roared at each other with their shark faces. They could feel that the door was starting to give way. They were exultant. They would have been infinitely patient; if the door had taken ten years to break down they would have given the time to it, but the moment of triumph was near. They sniffed the air with their blunt noses and scented blood. They charged again, running towards the door, heads down, noses forward. Three or four more good runs would do it.

They ran and braced their heads for the impact and hurtled forward, but when the blow came the door was a lot more yielding than they'd expected. It crumpled forward, giving no resistance. It had been unlocked from the inside. The door burst open, half off its hinges. Behind the desk, at the far end of the room, Jane Blythe was sitting, smiling faintly.

Symington and Blenkinsop crashed through into the room, stumbling and dazed. They focused on Jane and advanced, roaring. Behind them, Andrew and Sameera quietly tiptoed through the open door, into the outer office. Symington and Blenkinsop's faces morphed back into their polite, deadly human forms. They advanced on Jane.

'You have concealed wanton criminals,' said Mr Blenkinsop.

'Come now,' said Mr Symington, 'tell us where you've hidden them.'

'I'm afraid that we shall have to take matters into our own hands,' said Mr Blenkinsop.

'We have no other choice,' said Mr Symington, tipping his head to the side like a predator eyeing its prey.

'We usually try to be polite.'

'Courteous.'

'We go out of our way. But in a case like this…'

'I'm afraid,' said Mr Symington, 'that the gloves are off.'

His skin turned greyer and greyer.

'We have to go back and help,' whispered Sameera as Andrew dragged her past Jane's neatly ordered post-it notes towards the door of the outer office.

'There's nothing we can do,' whispered Andrew. 'We have to find the Doctor and tell him what's going on here.'

'But we—'

There was a piercing scream from the inner office.

'They're going to kill her! And she never even had one of the watches!'

'There's nothing we can do,' said Andrew. 'If we go back, they'll kill us too. Come on, before they find us!'

He put his arm around her shoulders and half-led, half-dragged her to the lift. And behind them there was a sound of screaming, eventually overwhelmed by the noise of crunching bones.

In the library of Lexington Bank's London office, workmen had set up a podium for the Chancellor of the Exchequer's visit. Chairs were lined up in rows. Beautifully bound presentation copies of the Bank's annual report were on each chair – someone had worked several nights at once to get those done in time. Television cameras were there too, trained on the podium where the Chancellor would deliver his speech. And behind the stage, an urgent whispered conversation was taking place.

'It was horrible,' said Sameera. 'We could hear them eating her.'

'How can they do that, Doctor?' asked Andrew. 'I thought they had to work according to contracts? If you never borrowed from them, they couldn't touch you. I thought… I thought it was all our fault.'

Sameera caught his hand and squeezed it for a moment.

'Sounds like they've changed the way they operate,' said the Doctor. 'Plus, have you noticed that none of them are anywhere about?'

'Yeah, we noticed,' said Andrew. 'We expected they'd follow us, thought we'd be on the run like all of you.'

He looked around. The thin orange glowing-pencil line was drawn around the Doctor, Rory and Amy from Nadia's watch. Sameera and Andrew had taken the change in Nadia quite well, considering.

'You brought a child with you... to a bank full of aliens?' Sameera had asked.

'I'm not a child, I'm the Head of Marketing,' Nadia had said, and Sameera had stared at her, then shrugged, deciding to accept it.

'Do you think they're planning something, Doctor?' asked Rory.

The Doctor shrugged.

'Probably. They've probably already planned something.'

He peeped round the black material forming the backdrop of the stage.

The television crew were testing their equipment.

'One two, one two,' said a woman into a microphone. 'Did you pick that up OK, Steve?'

The Doctor turned his attention to the centre of the atrium, with its great twisted-glass sculpture. He stared up at it.

'So we all know what we're here to do, right?' said Amy.

Rory nodded. 'We have to let the world know what's going on, before everyone's wearing those watches.'

Lexington Bank employees started to file into the

hall. The place was going to be packed. No one would be able to tell who was supposed to be here and who wasn't.

'Time for our cue, then,' said Andrew.

'Let's go,' said Sameera, and they walked towards their positions near to the podium.

From the other side of the fabric backdrop, two men in smart suits listened to the conversation, watched Andrew and Sameera walk in and take up their seats on the aisle in front of the stage.

'How very interesting, don't you think, Mr Symington?'

'A conversation with an invisible entity.'

'Partially visible, Mr Symington, partially visible.'

'Quite so. Intermittently perceptible, intermittently quite vanished.'

'Curious.' Mr Blenkinsop tipped his head to the side. 'Do you think that this could have anything to do with this Doctor, of whom we have heard so much?'

'So much, Mr Blenkinsop, but not nearly enough.'

'I certainly think we need to hear a great deal more about him.'

'And to see him. Really to come to understand him.'

'Indeed. My guess is that he will make a very valuable acquaintance for us.'

'Very valuable indeed,' said Mr Symington, smiling.

Chapter 17

As his car drove past St Paul's Cathedral, the Chancellor of the Exchequer was running through his final notes. It had been a good year so far, broadly speaking. After the first six months of 2007, the economy was booming, the City was doing well, and Lexington Bank was a model of efficiency and work-life balance. The Chancellor was pleased. The Bank would be the perfect place, and this the perfect time, for a speech about Britain's sustainable economic future and the end of the cycle of boom and bust. He checked the time with his aide. They were a couple of minutes ahead of schedule. Marvellous. An hour to deliver the speech now, after that a meeting with the Prime Minister, then an early dinner before tackling some of those red boxes. Plus, his wife had mentioned some wonderful watch she'd picked up that she was longing to show him that evening.

The car pulled up outside the back entrance of Lexington Bank. The Senior Vice-President of the London office was there to greet him – Vanessa Laing-Randall had unfortunately been called away on urgent business. But everything else was running like clockwork. A brief set of handshakes. A photoshoot with the Bank's in-house photographer. A few moments behind the curtain at the back of the stage to make sure his notes were in the right order and wonder, very briefly, who that odd man in the tweed jacket was. And then an arm at his elbow, a muttered 'This way, Chancellor, don't trip on the cable,' and the bright lights of the TV cameras and a speech to deliver.

Loitering by the television cameras – and flirting idly with the cameramen – Amy waited for the red light that meant 'live' to go on. The Doctor had told her she could get a few metres away from Nadia without the Symingtons and Blenkinsops being able to see her, but not much further than that. It was all right – she didn't have to go far, and she'd worked out what she was going to do.

The light went red. The cameraman cocked his finger by his ear and pointed to the Chancellor at the podium. It was only live on the Parliamentary News channel, but as soon as they'd heard what Amy had to say, the story would be all around the world.

'I'm delighted,' the Chancellor was saying, 'to speak today at Lexington Bank, a model of how banks across the world should run their business and a symbol of what makes London the greatest financial centre on Earth. The commitment shown by Lexington to employee welfare, and the value it generates for the economy...'

Amy suddenly broke away from the cameraman and sprinted down the main aisle. No one tried to stop her – all the dignitaries and senior bank officials in the aisle seats were too puzzled by what was happening to react quickly enough. The Chancellor stumbled slightly in his speech but gamely tried to continue as Amy leapt up in front of him at the podium.

'The City of London is the great powerhouse of our economy,' he read, 'and as such it is fitting that...'

'It's all lies!' shouted Amy. 'Aliens have taken over – they're giving out watches like these,' she rolled up her sleeve to show the watch.

'Get her down!' shouted someone. 'Security!'

Two besuited men who'd been standing quietly behind the Chancellor of the Exchequer took him gently by the elbows and guided him out through the curtain to the waiting limousine – they'd been well briefed for events like this. The cameraman was looking for instruction from a producer standing by. Amy realised that to the millions of people watching the television right now she must sound insane.

'Look!' she said.

Nadia was lurking at the side of the stage. Amy hauled the 10-year-old girl out in front of the lights. Two security guards were thundering across the atrium towards the gathered visitors. Rory and Andrew stepped out smartly to head them off. Andrew tripped one up with a chair, Rory started shouting at the other one about something happening behind him – enough to confuse them for a moment.

'Nadia, tell them what happened to you!'

Nadia looked straight into the eye of the camera.

She pulled down her sleeve so that her blistered arm with the sparks still flying out of the watch were clearly visible.

'Six months ago,' she said, 'I was 40 years old. But I was stupid. I borrowed time using this device. Look at me now.' She shook her wrist angrily. 'Just look at me.'

They never knew whether it was the shaking that had done it, or whether the watch, always fragile and malfunctioning, was never going to last much longer. But as Nadia shook her hand at the camera, as the security guards reached up to pull Amy from behind the podium, Nadia's watch gave out a final spurt of sparks, made a gentle sighing noise and a series of short clicks. Its face went dead. Nadia stared at it with horror.

The thin protective orange shield around Amy collapsed. All around the atrium, and in all the offices looking out onto it, dozens of heads turned instantly towards Amy. They were all Symingtons and Blenkinsops. Like predators scenting blood, their faces turned towards her – blank, unsmiling, with very sharp teeth indeed.

Sameera could see what was happening. She watched the Symingtons and Blenkinsops approaching Amy, who was blinded by the TV lighting.

There were only seconds left. This was the last opportunity to show the world, and Sameera was going to take it. She ran up onto the podium.

'Look!' she said into the TV camera. 'If you don't believe her, watch this. I'm going to pay back the time I've borrowed – just watch!'

Sameera looked into the lens of the camera, a

measured and thoughtful look. She brought her watch up in front of her face. She pressed the payment button.

She felt thirty-five years heap upon her body, all the accumulated damage of that amount of time, all the sore joints and the stiffened sinews and the aching muscles and the thousand different tiny pains one learns to live with over the years, all of them descending on her in one cataclysmic moment. She would have screamed, but she didn't have the strength in her. She noticed her wrinkled hands as she clung to the podium for support. She kept looking at the camera.

'This is what they've done,' she said. 'And now they're coming for us.'

It was instinct, it seemed. Not calculated, not well thought out. It was the instinct of a cat unable to stop itself twitching towards the cotton reel on a string. The Symingtons and Blenkinsops began to run, loping towards Amy in a single amalgamating pack, a body of animals scenting the hot sharp smell of fear. The security guards were helpless now, washed away by the tide of Symingtons and Blenkinsops.

Amy backed away, pulling Nadia with her, back behind the curtain, as Rory on one side of the podium and Andrew and Sameera on the other side tried to fight off the business-suited men closing in from all directions.

Behind the curtain, Amy found the Doctor using his sonic screwdriver on the scaffolding structure holding the curtain in place.

'That was very good, Pond, very succinct, warning the nation, very direct I thought, you could go into politics maybe, if the whole… professional kisser thing doesn't work out.'

'Doctor, they're coming!'

'I know,' he said nonchalantly. 'You push over there, I'll push here.'

He indicated a spot at the far end of the scaffolding. Amy leaned on the weak point and pushed with all her might. The Doctor heaved too, and the whole structure toppled gracefully forward, carrying the billowing black fabric down. It fell onto nine or ten of the approaching shark-men. Amy could see them struggling under the swathes of cloth.

But more were coming. Rory was ready with his camera, trying to get them as they came through the door, and the resulting bubbles full of Symingtons and Blenkinsops blocked the entrance a bit, but of course the bubbles popped unexpectedly, and there were more coming, always more and more.

Andrew and Sameera were fighting hand to hand. The Symingtons and Blenkinsops weren't hard to take down, weren't particularly tough. They threw chairs and lighting equipment at them, trying constantly to keep them back. Sameera was weaker now than she had been, but still summoned the strength to hurl a piece of camera equipment at an approaching Symington. She hit it in the mouth, and immediately half the other Symingtons in the room had bloody lips and a chipped tooth. Sameera stared for a moment before she got it.

'If you hurt one, they all get hurt!' she shouted.

Rory kicked viciously at the knee of the Blenkinsop advancing on him. Several of the other Blenkinsops started to limp with varying degrees of severity.

Sameera stamped on the toes of the one nearest to her, and several others winced.

But there were too many of them, they were coming too quickly, they were attacking from all directions and seemed increasingly able to predict what would happen before it happened.

'They're remembering!' shouted the Doctor, as one of the Blenkinsops perfectly dodged a large piece of expensive-looking video equipment Rory had thrown at it, and the Symington behind him caught it and threw it back.

'Look! Look at those ones at the edges!'

There were two Symingtons and Blenkinsops standing around the sides of the library. They looked less battle-weary than the others – their clothes were immaculate, there were no scratches on their faces. All the others were becoming increasingly bruised and battered from the fight, but the ones at the edges were fine.

'They're the earliest ones!' shouted the Doctor. 'Whatever they see, all the others remember!'

He feinted jumping to the left, behind a bookcase, but instead jumped up onto the desk.

'Target those ones with your camera, Rory! That'll slow them down!'

Rory turned the camera towards the Symingtons and Blenkinsops at the edge. But as he looked, the screen started to flash. 'WARNING,' it said, 'ONLY ONE LUCKY ROMANCE MOMENT REMAINING. CHOOSE CAREFULLY YOUR SWEETHEART TIMES!'

He hesitated, looking around for where he could get the most Symingtons and Blenkinsops in one camera bubble. And was this even the best moment to use it, he asked himself. Mightn't they have more urgent need for it later? So hard to know…

They knew he'd hesitate, of course, they'd seen him do it already. And when he paused for a moment, staring at the back of his camera, three Blenkinsops leapt forward, pushed Rory to the ground, and grabbed Amy.

Amy struggled, screaming and kicking under the grip of the Blenkinsop who was holding her. Its mouth peeled back. Far too wide, far wider than any head should be able to open. The enormous mouth began to lower over Amy's shoulder.

'No!' shouted Rory.

A Symington put a hand on Rory's shoulder. How had they all got so close, so quickly?

'The terms of her contract are very clear,' said Mr Symington. 'She agreed to the contract. The terms must be fulfilled.' He pulled Amy's wrist out and tapped at her watch. The illuminated display flashed in the air: 'BORROWED TIME TOTAL: 21 YEARS, 1 MONTH, 16 DAYS.'

'But, but… contracts can be renegotiated.' Rory's speech was choked. He took a deep breath. 'Take me instead.'

The Blenkinsop looked at Rory, a sullen unblinking expression on its shark-face.

'Rory, no,' said Amy.

'We're married,' said Rory, softly, as though she were the only other person in the room. 'Your debts are my debts.' He stared at the Blenkinsop. 'Her debts are my debts. Take me.'

'No, Rory,' said Amy. 'You can't… you can't… It's

twenty years of your life, Rory, you can't...'

He shrugged and managed a lopsided smile. 'You've always liked an older man –' he indicated the Doctor with a tip of his head – 'you might even like me better twenty years older.'

Blenkinsop looked between Rory and Amy. Its teeth retracted, its head became more human. 'This transaction is legal according to the stipulations in the terms and conditions,' it said.

Rory held out his arm. The Blenkinsop let Amy go. It walked towards Rory, hands reaching out. Rory took a deep breath. Twenty years paid off all in one go was going to hurt. He closed his eyes. He didn't see the Doctor step deftly in front of him.

'I don't think so,' said the Doctor to the Blenkinsop.

'Doctor,' said Rory. 'There's nothing you can do, we'll work something out, they can't take it from Amy, she's...'

'I think you'll find,' said the Doctor to the Blenkinsop, 'that your boss won't be interested in these small fry any more, when you tell her...' He took a deep breath. 'When you mention to her that I'm familiar with the Time Market.'

And all the noise of fighting fell away, and all the Symingtons and Blenkinsops were still and silent. And the lift doors binged.

Vanessa Laing-Randall stalked out of the elevator.

'What the hell is going on here?' she shouted. 'Who are all these people? And, might I add, who are *you*, Doctor? I just had a phone call from the Doctor Schmidt we were expecting from Zurich – he's been unavoidably detained. So who the hell are you, and what are you doing in my bank?'

'We know what you've been doing!' Rory shouted at Vanessa. 'We know everything about the watches, lending time, your loan sharks! We know everything, and we're going to stop you!'

Vanessa looked at Rory with a mixture of anger and bewilderment. 'I have literally no idea what you're babbling about,' she said.

'We know why the office's work productivity has increased 300 per cent since you got here,' shouted Andrew.

Vanessa looked, if anything, even more confused.

'I'm a highly efficient manager,' she said. 'Operational savings, cost analysis, motivation. The raft of measures I've introduced mean that—'

'There's no use lying any more!' said Sameera, 'Everyone can see what you've done to me.'

Vanessa blinked. 'Done to you? I don't even know you. I don't have any idea what you're talking about.'

The Doctor looked at Vanessa. 'No,' he said. 'I know you don't.'

He took a step towards the lift that Vanessa had walked out of. Its doors were still open. There was someone in there, someone small and quiet just waiting, half hidden in the lift.

'But you do, don't you, Jane?' he shouted.

Jane Blythe, the personal assistant, stepped out of the shadows.

'I did wonder,' she said, 'how long it would take you to work that one out.'

Chapter 18

Vanessa stared at Jane, her loyal assistant, the woman who'd worked tirelessly to help her rise to the top. She thought of all the times she'd been stumped for the perfect idea for a pitch only to find that Jane had happened to collate all the relevant documents for her in good time. Of how Jane seemed able to do five days' work in an afternoon. Of how tireless she was, how dedicated.

'Jane,' she said, 'what is going *on*? Do you know these people? Is this some kind of management training exercise I don't understand?'

'Oh, do shut up,' spat Jane.

Vanessa, who had never been spoken to like that in her life, shut up.

'You can let them all go now,' said the Doctor, gently. 'You and I could just talk about what you're doing here – necessary business practices I'm sure – and your sharks,' he motioned with his head toward the creature holding Amy, 'could stand down.'

'Oh, Doctor,' said Jane. 'You really haven't the faintest idea what's going on here, have you? You're as foolish as Vanessa.'

'How dare you—' began Vanessa.

'Did you really think it was all you?' said Jane. 'Your leadership, your motivation, your clever little time-saving tips? Emails about updating your to-do list while brushing your teeth? Tricks for managing effective meetings?'

'I've been highly praised by head office for my motivational techniques. I—'

'You know nothing. Less than nothing. Did you really think that your motivational techniques could make people do ten days' work in an afternoon? Did you really imagine that *you* were the magic factor that turned this office into a productivity machine in six months?'

Vanessa really had thought so. 'Yes,' she said. 'I...' And then she couldn't think of anything to follow it up with, so she shut up again.

'You are without doubt,' Jane said, 'one of the most self-satisfied, wilfully blind, arrogant, greedy people it has ever been my great delight to parasitise. You have been the perfect cover for me, and now I don't need you any more.'

'Now just wait a second!' said Vanessa.

'You don't have to do this!' shouted the Doctor.

'Oh, Doctor,' said Jane. 'I don't have to. But I want to.'

One of the Symingtons put its hand very politely on Vanessa shoulder. Its jaws were slightly open, its triangular teeth visible.

'You can't... you can't do anything to me,' said Vanessa. 'I never wore one of these watches.'

'But you saw people wearing them, didn't you?' said Jane. 'You saw and you said nothing, and you didn't want to know. No one ever wants to know how the money is made, only that they're making more.'

'But I... you can't do anything to me without a contract.'

Jane smiled, thinly, and withdrew a slim document from her jacket pocket. 'Did you ever think to read all the correspondence I asked you to sign? Did you ever stop to look at the little "sign here" flags and wonder what you were agreeing to?'

She unfolded the paper. It was headed 'Contract for the transfer of time,' and Vanessa Laing-Randall's signature was clear at the bottom.

Vanessa started to squirm in the Symington's grasp. 'You can't!' she said. 'Not after everything I've done for you, not after we rose to the top together. You can't forget all that and—'

'Jane, don't do it this way,' said the Doctor. 'Don't—'

'Unless you want it to be Amy instead, Doctor, you'll keep your mouth shut,' said Jane. 'You never had the slightest idea what was going on,' she said to Vanessa, as the Symington's shark teeth closed on Vanessa's shoulder and her skin began to wrinkle. 'After all, a good PA always knows more than her boss.'

Vanessa's screams rose higher and thinner, turned into a little wailing squeak and then, as her desiccated body twitched under the Symington's bite, into a tiny sigh. The husk fell to the floor, light and dry as sand.

There was a long silence in the atrium.

At last, Sameera said: 'You tricked us. We tried to help you, and you tricked us.'

'Oh, you do catch on fast,' said Jane.

'You can't win!' shouted Sameera. 'Everyone in the world has seen this broadcast! Everyone knows what you're doing now – no one will borrow any more time from you.'

Jane looked at Sameera's wrinkled face. 'Time hasn't been kind to you, my dear.'

Andrew put his arm around Sameera's shoulders.

'You can't fool anyone now,' he said. 'This broadcast has gone worldwide.'

Jane shook her head. 'Oh,' she said, 'I'm afraid not. You see, one or two of us heard what you were about to do. We blocked the transmission. The only people who saw your noble gesture were the people in this building. You can't stop me that way, I'm afraid. We will always be one step ahead of you. Time travel – makes plots so very difficult to foil.'

Andrew stood with his arms around Sameera as she stared ahead, blinking hard to keep the tears back.

'Now, Doctor.' Jane smiled thinly. 'What was that you were saying to my esteemed colleagues here about the Time Market?'

'Do you really mean "colleagues"? It's just that I was beginning to suspect that…'

'You're very perspicacious.'

'You're all the same organism, aren't you? Head and tails, or rather in your case tail and heads. Are you the earliest?'

Jane smiled. The Symingtons and Blenkinsops smiled too, unnerving grins breaking out on a hundred scarred and bruised faces.

'Too, too clever. I shall be delighted to discover

exactly where you found all this out… and then go back in time to make sure you never find it out in the first place. Yes, I'm the first. These are all my… what can I call us?'

'Tendrils?' volunteered a Symington.

'Fronds?' suggested a Blenkinsop.

'Appendages?' offered another.

'Excrescences?' said yet another.

'Something like that,' said Jane, patting a Symington gently on the arm. 'I am a tree trunk and these are the branches. Aren't they lovely? Back and forth, back and forth in time, constantly growing and expanding, each new one remembering everything the previous ones have experienced. Does it get boring, dears?'

'Not at all,' smiled the Symington, 'we all work together for the good of the team, wasn't that Vanessa Laing-Randall's motto?'

'Quite right. We're all,' said Jane, 'exceptionally good team players. Now, back to that delicious thing you mentioned earlier, Doctor.'

'Treacle tart? Did I say treacle tart? I can't remember if I did, though treacle tarts are delicious. Nice sculpture you've got there,' said the Doctor, staring at the glass shape in the atrium. 'I've kept on wondering what it was about it that appealed to me so much, and now I think I begin to understand. Because you haven't actually called in much of the time you're owed, have you? You haven't—'

A Blenkinsop grabbed Amy's left arm and twisted it behind her back until she screamed out.

'Time Market,' said Jane again. 'Do go on, I have all the time in the world.'

The Doctor stared at Jane. He turned to look at Rory, still brandishing his camera, and Amy struggling in the Blenkinsop's grip.

'Rory, Amy,' he said. 'You know I trust you implicitly.'

'Doctor?' said Rory, in a worried tone.

'If I tell you what I know, Jane,' said the Doctor, 'will you forgive Amy's debt? Will you let her go free?'

'Well that depends, Doctor, on what you've got to tell. After all, she has racked up quite substantial borrowings.' Jane tapped on her smartphone and drew in breath sharply over her teeth. 'Twenty-five years, goodness me. Do you think you could pay that off for her, Doctor?'

The Doctor shrugged. 'If I promise to pay it off and tell you what I know, will you let her go?'

Jane shrugged. 'I don't see why not. Now tell me.'

'First let her go.'

The Blenkinsop holding Amy dragged her over to the Doctor and held out her watch arm to him.

'To indicate that you are paying off this being's time debts and agree to assume those debts yourself, press here.'

A button on the watch illuminated.

'Careful, Doctor,' said Jane. 'Twenty-five years all in one go can smart, you know.'

The Doctor looked Jane directly in the eye and pressed the button.

Amy's watch strap undid itself.

The watch fell to the floor, the glass face shattered on the marble tiles.

The Doctor didn't flinch.

'But you...' Jane blinked, unsure of herself for the

first time since she'd revealed herself. She took a pace towards him. 'You didn't age.'

The Doctor looked uncomfortable. He said nothing. Amy wondered if he'd revealed too much.

All the Symingtons and Blenkinsops were staring at the Doctor now. Rory noticed that all of them were breathing in unison. In and out, in and out. Chests rising and falling, breathing fast with excitement.

Jane walked up to the Doctor, touched the cuff of his sleeve, the back of his hand with a light, reverent gesture.

'It can't be. They told me all of you were gone,' she said. 'They swore there were none left and never would be or would have been, ever again.'

'Hey,' said the Doctor, snatching his hand away, 'don't paw. And don't believe everything you hear.'

'You're a…'

The Doctor shrugged. 'Yeah, I know. Unicorn.'

Jane's voice was a dazed whisper. 'Time Lord. I did not think to live so long.'

The Symingtons and Blenkinsops rearranged themselves on the floor of the building. It wasn't that they moved. It was more that they had suddenly always been in these new positions. Across the exits, flanking Jane, all of them facing the Doctor, as if they couldn't bear to look at anything else.

'Doctor, what's going on?' asked Amy.

The Doctor smiled at her. 'I think our friend the Time Harvester here has just worked out how to make a killing on the market.'

'A mere formality, Doctor,' said Jane. 'You and I both

understand that no physical prison can hold you. It would be as if a two-dimensional creature drew a circle around your feet and imagined that it had trapped you.'

'Oh, I wouldn't say that,' said the Doctor. 'All depends on what kind of locks they put on.'

'But you…'

The Doctor sighed. 'Come on, then. Enough of the standing around gawping. I'm not a circus freak. Let's see… I don't know, will you let Andrew here go if I wear one of your watches?'

'You would wear… I don't understand.'

'Can't see how to make it any simpler. Andrew owes you a notional 55,000 years, probably gone up a bit in the past few hours actually, how long has it been since we checked Andrew? Five hours? Maybe you owe them 100,000 years, these things mount up quickly. So let's say, you put a watch on me, tap directly into my time stream, and in exchange you forgive Andrew his debt? And then we'll talk about the rest of the human race – obviously I'm not going to undervalue myself.'

'I…' Jane opened and closed her mouth a couple of times, then motioned to a Symington, who, very gently and cautiously, as if expecting some kind of trap, took a watch from his pocket and fastened it around the Doctor's wrist. Andrew's watch strap unfastened itself – he just managed to catch it before it hit the floor.

'I'll take that I think, Andrew,' said the Doctor, and put Andrew's discarded watch around his right wrist.

'Doctor, what are you doing?' muttered Amy.

The Doctor shrugged. 'At least you're all free now. The Symingtons and Blenkinsops can't do anything to you at all now you don't owe them time. Well, they can attack you, but they can't just suddenly take away all your time. And…' the Doctor motioned to the huge glass sculpture and dropped his voice very low, so that only Amy could hear 'and I suspect that may be what Sameera would call a liquidity fund. You can work out the rest. I don't know what you'll do without me, Amy,' he said, raising his voice again, 'but I know that whatever it is, it'll be *smashing*.'

A Symington and a Blenkinsop put a cold hand on each of the Doctor's shoulders.

'You really must come with us now, Doctor,' said Jane. 'I know some people who'll be very excited to see you.'

Amy had felt broken-hearted before. Miserable, even depressed. But there was no feeling she could imagine worse than the desolate hollowness of watching Jane and her Symington-and-Blenkinsop army lead the Doctor away across the atrium.

'Where do you think they're taking him?' muttered Rory.

Amy shrugged.

At the far end of the atrium, a Blenkinsop patted the Doctor down with surprising courtesy. Blenkinsop removed several objects from the Doctor's pockets and put them on the floor. He turned back to Jane and nodded.

Amy had expected the escort party to turn out into the street, or perhaps summon a spaceship or something. But, she realised, she'd been thinking three-dimensionally again – an annoying habit of her brain. As they reached the far side of the building, Jane turned a dial on the Doctor's watch, and they all just vanished. In the spot where they'd been was just a small heap of the Doctor's belongings – an apple, some string, a swanee whistle and the sonic screwdriver.

'Doesn't matter where they're taking him,' said Amy, staring down at the sad little heap. 'I think the important question is: "When?"'

The building was all but deserted now. The street had been cordoned off by the police, who were interviewing the security guards, the people responsible for the outside broadcast and senior staff. No one was bothering about anyone junior – a lot of people had left. Even if Sameera's self-sacrificing act had only been broadcast to the televisions in conference rooms around the building, it had been enough for everyone who'd borrowed time to understand that something bad was going on. And almost everyone who hadn't borrowed any still understood that there'd been a massive fight at the Chancellor's speech, and that this probably meant that no one would notice if they sneaked off a bit early to deal with something vital like spending time with their children, sleeping for more than four consecutive hours or seeing someone about those recurrent chest pains.

The Symingtons and Blenkinsops seemed mostly to have gone too – apart from a few dozen stationed at key points around the building, Amy, Rory, Sameera and Andrew found that they could walk the halls mostly without being disturbed. But instead they sat in Andrew's office disconsolately.

'He's given us a mission,' said Amy.

'He could be dead,' said Rory.

'He's not dead,' said Amy.

'He could be…'

'I'd know,' said Amy. 'If he was dead, I'd know. OK? And he's not.'

Andrew looked out of his window at the glass sculpture in the atrium.

'So we're supposed to, what, destroy some advanced alien technology?' said Andrew. Amy noticed that Andrew's hand was still casually resting on Sameera's shoulder. Even though she was about 65 now – that was some kind of friendship.

'And what good is it going to do? She's got the Doctor,' said Rory.

Amy shrugged.

'The Doctor said something about a "liquidity fund",' she said, 'but I don't know what that is.'

Andrew and Sameera looked at each other.

'A… liquidity fund…' murmured Andrew.

'It makes sense,' said Sameera.

'What is it?' said Rory.

'No, look,' said Sameera. 'Jane hasn't called in all the debts yet, right? Most people are still wearing the watches and walking around perfectly normally. They might owe 55,000 years –' Andrew grimaced – 'but so far they haven't *had* to repay a minute, right?'

'Right.'

'So it's like she kind of "has" that time – in the sense that people owe it to her – but she can't use it because she hasn't actually taken it. It's sort of… frozen. Solid. Can't move like a liquid.'

'Right!' said Amy, finally understanding. 'So how is she moving through time? How are the Symingtons and

Blenkinsops able to fold back on themselves in time? She can't be doing all that with the few accounts she's called in.'

'She must have some time stored up already,' said Andrew. 'Maybe she had it before, maybe she's borrowed it from somewhere else, some kind of Time Market? It doesn't matter – the point is she needs a pool of time that she can actually use. Which is a liquidity fund.'

'So if we smashed it…' said Amy, 'I don't know how, we'll work that out, but if we smashed it somehow…'

'It wouldn't affect the fact that loads of people still owe her time,' said Sameera.

'But it could cause her some problems moving around, might get rid of a few Symingtons and Blenkinsops even,' said Andrew.

'A liquidity crisis,' said Sameera, 'can be very nasty.'

'But seriously, it's going to be protected, isn't it?' said Rory.

Sameera nodded. 'He's got a point. It is advanced technology.'

'Really advanced,' said Andrew. 'We don't understand how any of the bits of it work.'

'What's that on your desk?' said Amy.

Andrew glanced over to his desk. His beloved eBook reader was sitting in its protective sleeve on top of a pile of papers. He'd saved up for that reader and the envious looks it got from other commuters gave him great joy.

'My eBook reader?' he said.

'Do you know how it works?' said Amy.

'I… um… it's a computer? And a touchscreen?'

'But you don't know how any of the bits of it work, not on the inside?'

Andrew shook his head.

'But that's different, that's...'

Amy reached over and grabbed the eBook reader. She held it above her head with both hands and before any of the others had time to react, she brought it down hard on the edge of the desk.

There was a loud crunching bang. The screen smashed into crazed fragments. Tiny pieces of glass flew across the desk. Amy flipped the reader back over in her hands. The screen was half-detached in one corner. It was totally destroyed. Andrew stared at her with disbelieving wide eyes.

'Just because you don't know how something works,' she said, 'doesn't mean you can't break it. And don't look at me like that,' she said to Andrew. 'You borrowed 55,000 years from some aliens. That reader was just collateral damage. Come on, let's go and break some glass.'

Chapter 19

The view on the monitors was dark. Occasionally, a line of numbers scrolled past, faster than any human eye could have followed them. But mostly, it was dark. It was dark, in a sense, all the time. But then, 'all the time' is a relative concept. A lot can happen in a slice of time too infinitesimally small to be measured on any human scale. So, occasionally there was a burst of frenetic activity. But mostly, it was dark.

The monitors were set up around a central well, which was empty. Well, mostly it was empty. Occasionally, for an infinitely tiny period of time, it was more full than would have been possible if some very advanced trans-dimensional physics weren't being used.

Officially, no one had stood in that hall – with its huge glass domes radiating a tiny amount of light, and the enormous tall arched windows with their view of three blood-red moons – for a very long time. Everything that had ever happened there had happened in the past. There were occasional checks and monitors to make sure that remained the case. A cordon in time had been placed around it.

But time travel is sadly far more complicated than that, and even the Shadow Proclamation had failed fully to understand what a very clever team of experts with extremely advanced degrees were able to do by repackaging time. A vast amount of time engineering and accountancy had gone into making sure that everything that would ever happen here stayed in the past.

Once you can slow down time, almost anything is possible.

The market was due to be open between 24:26:95:01:03 and 24:26:95:01:04, Galactic Standard time. This meant a certain amount of preparation. For subjective days, the participants had been arriving or setting up their remote links. The market operators – strictly hush-hush, there was nothing remotely legal about this operation – had been setting up the rules of operation. They'd taken their time over it. At least two additional milliseconds on either side of the market open window. They'd heard there was something special coming in. They'd wanted to make a fuss.

So, at the appointed moment, there was a raised platform made of glass in the centre of the trading floor. And around the raised platform were rows and rows of glass bricks, each one with a warm beating movement at its centre. The ripple of owed time slowly accumulating. Most of the beings in this room could read a glass brick as easily as Andrew Brown could have read a newspaper. These blocks read very well indeed. There was time to be made here, they could feel it. And that was before the star attraction was shown to the crowd.

On the raised platform was a thin glass sheet. A screen, viewable from both sides. And, in the brief millisecond that the whole place became alive with traders, the screen flickered into life. And all the little screens around the outside turned on too. They all showed the same image, broadcast from a storage room under the Millennium Dome in London, Earth. It was a man, fastened to a time-harvesting device, held at the throat and the wrists and the ankles. The room drew a quick, sharp breath. Some of them had enough residual instinct to know what they were looking at before the voice came over the speakers and told them.

'This,' said the voice of the thing that had called itself Jane Blythe, 'is the last of the Time Lords.'

Her face came into view at the edge of the screen, a thin smile on her lips.

'The very last Time Lord to survive the Time War,' she said. 'What am I bid?'

And then a great clamour rose up from the creatures in the pit, a sort of wailing, aching, sobbing shout, something between grief and desire and mad excited hysteria. And the trading began.

There was an inevitable flurry of early bids. That was only natural. It wasn't even clear whether Jane Blythe wanted to sell the Time Lord, but a good round of early bidding would give a rough idea of what buyers were willing to pay for him – an estimate of value. They settled at around five inhabited galaxies – about fifteen sextillion lives – before anyone even bothered to ask the obvious questions.

'What's the mileage of this Time Lord? How do we even know he is one?' came the message over the wires from several of the highest bidders at once.

It was unlikely that anyone would try to cheat the market – the penalties were too severe, the price exacted, in both directions in time, too high for many to try. But a Time Lord? One slightly used Time Lord? The possible rewards might be enough to make someone young enough and stupid enough give it a go.

'How did you find him?' they said.

'What did you pay for him?' one asked.

'Where can we get another one?' someone joked.

And eventually an Old Member of the market, someone who remembered how it had been long ago asked a question. This member could still recall when the market had sold regenerations piled high like apples on a grocer's stall, when renegade Time Lords – and there had been a few – had risked a great deal to purchase dirty time in this highly respectable chamber. This Old Member typed a request into a keypad with a yellowed claw. It flashed up on the screen for all to see.

'Let the Time Lord speak,' it said.

This was extremely irregular. This was a market on which lives were bought and sold, yes, but amalgamated, in great slices, as if they'd been pressed together and turned into a pâté. No one wanted to see the individual people who made up those slices of life-terrine. No one wanted to hear them speak. Imagine if they objected! Of course, they should have done that before they agreed to sign whatever contract it had been to borrow whatever they'd borrowed at the expense of their very lives. No one whose life was traded on this market ever addressed the trading floor.

But this was a unique situation. A convocation was held, instantly, between a dozen different time-traders, the grand old beings of the market. And it was agreed. In this case – and seeing that the Time Harvester in question was using the Time Lord as collateral for her various borrowings even now – it seemed the most sensible course of action. The message was relayed.

'The Time Lord will speak.'

Some things are obvious when you think of them. So obvious that the moment you've thought them, it's hard to imagine how you managed not to see them before. Like seeing a face in the pattern of the curtains, like finding out you've been mispronouncing a word all your life. Like imagining that house prices will go on rising for ever, and basing all your financial calculations on that. Some vulnerabilities are invisible until you see them, and once you see them you can't begin to imagine how the people in charge haven't seen them too. You can't believe that they haven't already taken action to prevent anyone exploiting them. Some weaknesses in the system are so big that once you notice them, you can't see anything else.

'They must have thought of this,' said Andrew, grappling with a metal handle already slippery from sweat. 'They'll have put up a force field or something.'

'Put your back into it,' said Amy. She was directing operations, which Andrew noticed meant that she wasn't actually doing any of the lifting. Even Sameera and 10-year-old Nadia were carrying a couple of metal drawers each. 'We've got to get it done fast or they'll all see us and come back to now and stop us.'

'But,' said Rory, heaving on the rope he'd nicked from the mailroom and slung around the filing cabinet, 'as they're not here, doesn't that mean they definitely don't come and stop us?'

Amy gave him one of her devastating wide-eyed hard stares. 'Doesn't work like that,' she said, 'and you know it. If they come back, we'll just have two memories of right now. Or something. And anyway, they might be back at any time, so heave!'

There was no way to get to the glass sculpture from below, that was certain. Nadia had gone to check it out. A ring of Symingtons and Blenkinsops surrounded the sculpture, weaving and shifting like fish in water, blending into each other and re-separating again and again. But the sculpture reached its icy glass fingers up all the way to the eighth floor through the central atrium of the building. All the offices looked out onto it. And on the tenth floor – the executives' floor, abandoned now by all the staff – there was a huge round balcony looking down past all the floors onto the sculpture. An unguarded balcony with a waist-high rail.

Amy had stood at that rail when she'd seen Brian Edelman collapse. She'd looked down onto the sculpture, seen the tiny flickering movement at the centre of it. She'd wondered even then why no one had ever thrown a brick down on it. She just had that kind of brain.

'How much further?' panted Rory.

Amy squinted down the corridor, pouting.

'Maybe another six metres?'

Rory and Andrew groaned in unison.

'You can do it!' said Sameera, lending her muscles to give the filing cabinet another heave. They'd picked the biggest, heaviest one they could find. It'd be great at smashing stuff – not so easy to move, though.

'Come on,' said Nadia, 'or they'll find us!'

'Oh dear,' said Mr Blenkinsop, very softly, just behind her.

The conversation, of course, was not like a normal conversation. No creature that can travel in time would ever negotiate in a normal way. Why would you, when you can travel forwards to see what position the other side is going to negotiate from, and backwards to pre-empt them?

Questions were put, via the system. They were deemed unsuitable. They were changed, in the past, to something more satisfactory. Jane scrutinised the Doctor's answers, blocked him from replying in ways she thought would be unsatisfactory. They tried again. And again. And again. The same tiny piece of time – ask a question, get an answer – over and over again.

'Don't you get bored,' asked the Doctor, 'of trying to engineer one perfect moment in time? Can't you just wait and see what happens, like everyone else does?'

Jane shrugged. 'Time Lords always did abdicate their responsibility for almost everything. Why is it that you keep on pretending to be normal?'

'Not pretend,' said the Doctor. 'I've never pretended. Almost everyone in the universe lives forwards. One thing, then the next, then the next. No second chances, no revisiting. Always onwards. It's better, in the end. Something has to die for something new to be able to live. Like regeneration. How long have you been living this same old looped existence?'

She made her demand again: 'Prove to us that you're a Time Lord.'

'Shan't,' he said.

She went back and tried again.

They were surrounded, suddenly, by ever-multiplying Symingtons and Blenkinsops. The creatures were muttering to each other, some entirely human, some entirely shark, some between one state and the other.

'I do think,' said a Symington, 'that attempts to destroy private property must constitute a breach of contract.'

'And even if not,' said a Blenkinsop, 'we must do our civic duty.'

Amy looked round wildly. They were advancing up the corridor behind them and from both sides. They'd be on them in seconds.

'Rory! Throw me the camera!' shouted Amy. 'We haven't got any time!'

'There are too many of them!' shouted Rory. 'And there's only one picture left!'

Amy stared hard at him. 'I've got an idea.'

He threw her the camera, kicking a Symington hard in the shins as he did.

Amy grabbed the camera, but didn't point it towards the attacking Symingtons and Blenkinsops. She pointed it at herself, and at Rory, and at Andrew and Sameera and Nadia, and the filing cabinet. And she clicked the button, but she didn't release it. Instead, holding it down, she ran.

She ran forward, towards the rail around the balcony, not daring to look behind her to see if what she'd done was working. When she reached the balcony she held the camera out as far as she could over the rail and then dropped it. It hung in midair, suspended by its own Lucky Romance Time Bubble. She looked back. It had worked.

Instead of a spherical bubble, the camera had created a long wobbling tube, stretching from where Rory, Nadia, Andrew and Sameera were standing with the filing cabinet all the way to the balcony and over the rail so that the camera was hanging directly above the glass sculpture.

Outside the bubble, the Symingtons and Blenkinsops were gnashing their teeth in slow-motion fury. Of course, thought Amy, the camera prolonged moments, so things outside seemed to be slowed down. To the Symingtons and Blenkinsops they'd look as if they were working at a furious pace.

Rory and Andrew looked at the bubble tunnel around them.

'Wow,' said Rory. 'That is clever.'

'Amazing,' said Nadia, poking at the bubble with her foot, then her hand, then her tongue.

'I didn't know it'd work,' said Amy.

'Is that… alien technology again?' said Andrew.

'Nah,' said Amy. 'Earth, fifty-first century. Come on, put your back into it, it could collapse at any moment!'

'You've borrowed heavily from the market, haven't you?' said the Doctor in one of those many conversations that never happened.

Jane shrugged. 'Leverage. Now I've got you, I'll

make it all back and more.'

'That's how you can do all your time tricks. The time of everyone on Earth wouldn't have been enough to bring both of us back here. You've borrowed more time than those watch-contracts are actually worth.'

'Things are worth what people are willing to pay for them. Right now, the members of this market are willing to pay a lot for those contracts, and for you.'

The Doctor smiled and said nothing. They went back and Jane tried again.

In fact, there were three subjective hours before the camera's final time bubble collapsed. Enough time for Rory to start complaining, complain at full volume, and then get bored with complaining, that she'd made them drag the filing cabinet so fast. Enough time for Nadia to start amusing herself making paper chains with the contents of some of the files and then wonder out loud whether she'd have done it anyway or whether her brain was regressing. Enough time for Andrew and Sameera to have a long quiet chat which Rory did his best to make sure Amy didn't listen to by complaining loudly at her. Enough time, most importantly, for them to manoeuvre the filing cabinet over the guard-rail, so that it hung in mid air above the very fragile-looking glass sculpture.

They thought about trying to get the camera back. It hung just out of reach, producing occasional cheerful 'Super Lucky Romance Days!' messages on its screen and even playing a little tune which Amy was sure it had never done before – perhaps it was a feature introduced to distract from its short battery life. But they decided it was too dangerous to crawl out along the jelly-tube to fetch it. What if the force field collapsed just as they were suspended above the drop down to the ground floor?

'If cameras had feelings,' said Amy, 'I expect it'd be pleased to go out doing its duty for the future of Earth.'

When the bubble started to disintegrate, it seemed to happen both incredibly slowly and also too fast to take in.

They were looking at the Symingtons and Blenkinsops through the bubble-wall, watching their hypnotic slow-motion movement as if they were in an aquarium, or a shark cage.

'They're quite interesting, when you're not fleeing for your life,' said Rory, 'have you seen how they develop gills as they're changing into a shark head but they never need to be in water. Do you think—'

'Super Lucky Romance Moment almost over!' announced the camera in a cheery voice. 'Put pants on!'

'Did that always have a voice?' said Amy.

'Did it just say, "Put pants on"?' said Rory.

And then the wobbling orange mass surrounding them started to shimmer and decay, and the slow-motion shark-men outside started to speed up to real time and with a faint pop the bubble burst and the camera and the filing cabinet started to fall and the Symingtons and Blenkinsops were on them with a roar as loud as the ocean.

Everything happened at once.

Playing its happy little Lucky Romance Song, the camera tumbled down ten storeys of Lexington Bank, clattering against the side of the glass sculpture in honour of work-life balance before smashing on the marble of the ground floor into a thousand sprockets and tiny gears which UNIT would subsequently spend eighteen fruitless months trying to reconstruct.

A Symington and a Blenkinsop grabbed Amy. They held her down on the floor.

'You've been a great deal of trouble to us, Ms Pond,' said one.

'But you won't be any trouble any more,' said the other.

And Amy struggled and kicked and screamed and fought as Mr Blenkinsop brought his face down towards her and began to bite into her arm, taking great gulps of something that she realised now was more precious to her than blood and she felt herself getting weaker and saw the world growing darker. She cried for help, but Rory and Andrew and Sameera and even Nadia were also shark food now.

And very slowly, the filing cabinet poised on the edge of the rail teetered and overbalanced and fell. A dozen Symingtons and Blenkinsops tried to stop it but whatever they tried there just wasn't enough time. It rotated as it tumbled and the sharp corner of its top hit the glass sculpture first, putting a large crack in it. The filing cabinet bounced a little and came down with the full force of its long flat side on the top of one of the melted-wax-like fingers of the sculpture, crashing down into the centre of the thing, sending huge viciously sharp fragments of glass flying into the windows of the offices around it. And the cabinet fell forward, into the heart of the sculpture, utterly crushing the small flickering light at the centre of it, releasing a bolt of warm energy which blew out all the windows on the ground floor and made each of the 326 people left in the building about 17 months younger.

There was a sound like a million cardboard boxes being suddenly flattened. A loud, dull crump.

And all the Symingtons and all the Blenkinsops feeding off Rory and Amy and Nadia and Andrew and Sameera suddenly disappeared. As if they had never been there to begin with.

And, on the thin glass screen on top of that dais in the domed room, Jane stumbled. Under the implacable gaze of the blood-red moons, she blinked and stuttered and couldn't quite gather her thoughts. It was time.

'Traders of the Time Market,' said the Doctor on the screen to the eager jostling crowd.

Jane tried to pull herself back together, to go back to a point in time when she could stop him saying it. But she didn't have enough spare time capacity. She barely had enough to maintain her escape route, let alone the intricate time-doublings she usually operated in. She was singular, moving forward through time. Always onwards, no going back. The feeling made her gasp.

'Traders of the Time Market your attention please,' said the Doctor. 'I don't know what this woman has told you, but I would like to state very plainly that I am not a Time Lord.' He paused, smiled slightly: 'I don't even know what a Time Lord is.'

There was dead silence on the trading floor.

'He's lying!' Jane managed to croak out.

'I'm not, you know. In fact, she's the one who's lying and I can prove it. Take a look at the other wares she's got for sale on this market. Take a good look. See those glass bricks?'

There were glass bricks piled up around the Doctor. Some had been transported to the trading floor itself, some were in further storage compartments, and the traders could glance through the aggregated accounts of them on their video screens. The collective total was considerable.

'They look pretty impressive, don't they? Very healthy profits, almost no risk of any of the loans defaulting – she's going to be raking in time on those. But let's take a look at the account of… oh, I don't know, how about this watch that I happen to have in my pocket here, recording the debt of one Andrew Brown. He owes, what, 100,000 years?'

The Doctor held the watch up so they could all see its face. He was right, of course.

'That's not an unusual debt, I think you'll agree, not in the accounts Jane's been trading.'

The traders looked at their screens. One hundred thousand years was a hefty debt – but it was only about ten per cent of what Jane stated in her briefing documents was a normal human lifespan. The humans would have no trouble repaying – and if they did, the owner of the contract could always foreclose on their life. It was purely a business transaction, all very simple and above board.

'Now check your information systems.'

'No!' shouted Jane. 'No, don't! He's lying, don't listen to him, he's trying to distract you so he can get away.'

'Check your information systems,' the Doctor repeated. 'I know you tap into all the classified networks. Check what a normal human lifespan is.'

There was a moment's pause while a thousand claws

and tentacles and pseudopods tapped on their screens for the information.

There was another pause while they tried to understand what they were reading.

And, as they understood the absolute worthlessness of the assets Jane had been trading on the market, there was a rising cacophony of shouting voices calling out.

'Sell! Sell! Sell!'

Chapter 20

There hadn't been a run on a Time Market trader for as long as the longest memory on the floor of the exchange. None of them knew quite what would happen. Jane's worth on the market dipped lower and lower. The contracts she'd aggregated for sale became worthless, less than worthless – traders were paying other traders to take them off their hands, frightened of what might happen if they were still holding them when the day's trading came to an end.

But there was a protocol, of a sort. There came a moment – an elongated moment, of course, the whole thing had taken less than a second – where she could no longer honour her obligations to the market. Where her value on the market was so low that she could no longer even maintain the basic time-travel capacities to continue to trade. Where her whole self started to unravel as the things that she'd done ceased to have been done, and the Doctor saw that at the far end of the long storage unit some of the glass bricks were starting to disappear. The Symingtons and Blenkinsops who had put those watches onto those wrists had never now existed. Time was undoing itself.

Jane saw the dissolution too. She begged, via the screen, for trading to be halted, for the traders to believe her that yes, she had lied about the Earth lifespan, but she had a Time Lord here, a real Time Lord, probably the last one left alive, with a TARDIS of his own, and, if only she could get him to open it, she'd have access to all the time, all the time that there ever was or would ever have been – if they'd only just stop and listen, just listen.

But it was too late. The panic was spreading through the market, wild and unreasoning. If Jane had lied to them, if they'd believed her, if they hadn't spotted the fraud, what other lies might they have believed? Which others of these solid-gold assets were actually just pretty sparkling sand? They tried to sell, but no one was buying; they tried to call in old debts, but suddenly encountered doubt about whether the debt was worth as much as they'd thought.

And then, somehow, the Time Lord was free.

No one knew how it had happened. Someone said they thought they'd seen him shift one of his hands under the harvesting chair to find a small pen-like device concealed beneath the seat. But that was clearly impossible – he couldn't have hidden anything there himself, the place was well guarded. And as everyone else had been paying far more attention to their rapidly diminishing fortunes, the question of how he'd got free was never answered to anyone's satisfaction.

But free he was. Jane herself was barely able to move. She kept flickering in and out of time, growing fainter as her ability to manipulate time decreased. As the Doctor watched, she flicked out of existence in that room altogether. Just as if she'd never been able to be there at all.

The Doctor looked at the screen showing the chaos on the trading floor. He cleared his throat.

'Hello,' he said. 'I'm the Doctor. I'm here to help.'

And silence spread across the Time Market.

'I wouldn't usually,' he said. 'Usually I'd leave you to stew in your own juices – those of you who have juices, wouldn't want to insult any gaseous life forms, you know what I mean. Usually, I'd walk away. I've started doing that more since the Time War. Walking away. And we all know whose dirty little trade kept that war going when it should have encompassed far fewer aeons, don't we?' His voice was very low. 'We all know why your disgusting business was outlawed by the Shadow Proclamation centuries before it began.'

There was a brief muttering at this, a slight hint of protest. The Doctor spoke over it.

'But it so happens,' he said, 'that the lives of a planet I rather care about are mixed up in all this. So. I don't care if every single one of you goes to the wall. Send each other Time-rupt for all I care. But before you do, who'd like to sell me their remaining Earth time contracts for, let's say, one second a decade?'

The pause was shorter than it is possible to measure without a timepiece far in advance of Earth technology before the floods of offers to sell came in. And the Doctor was soon the proud owner of the few remaining glass bricks in the storage unit.

*

No one at Lexington Bank knew how the sculpture had been broken. To be honest, none of the senior executives quite knew who'd put it there to begin with. Some of them had hazy memories of something – more like dreams than memories really – echoes of something that might have happened, but which seemed so improbable that it wasn't worth mentioning at all.

Police officers arrived very quickly at the scene of the damage, roped it off in the name of something called Torchwood. Those officers then had a prolonged argument with soldiers from something called UNIT, who arrived twenty minutes later and claimed that they'd been instructed by the Prime Minister, acting on information provided by the Chancellor of the Exchequer, to take control of the area.

The senior staff at Lexington Bank decided that the best idea was to call it a suspected gas leak, which had caused both the explosion and the strange memories many of them had of the few days before the blast. Everyone in the office would have a week off, to recover, they announced.

Even those few who could remember – those who were still wearing time-harvester watches after the sculpture smashed – found that they could take the watches off now. That the faces read 'CONTRACT VOIDED'. That no matter how they fiddled with them, they'd only say that or, with a lot of tinkering, the words 'THE OWNER OF YOUR CONTRACT, "DOCTOR OF GALLIFREY", HAS CANCELLED YOUR DEBT' would flash up once before disappearing for ever.

On the top floor of the building, in an abandoned office filled with a shower of multicoloured post-it notes, five people were sitting. Two of them were a young married couple, one a man in his thirties, another a woman in her sixties, along with a 10-year-old girl. They had the look of people who'd slept on the floor for a night or two.

'It's been two days,' said Rory. 'We can't live here on sandwiches for ever.'

'You're welcome to come and stay with me,' said Andrew, 'just until we work out what to do.'

Amy shook her head. 'The TARDIS is here. He's coming back here. I know he is. Look what it said on all the watches of those people in your departments. He's coming back.'

'What if he can't?' said Rory. 'What if he's stuck on another planet or something. Look, it could be worse – we could be stuck on another planet! At least it's Earth. All right, we'll overlap with ourselves for a while, but it's fine... I don't think we should stay here much longer.'

Nadia kicked at some papers. She wasn't 10. She knew she wasn't 10. But her brain was working a bit like a 10-year-old brain, and she found herself getting bored more often with these stupid conversations.

'What am I going to do?' she said. 'I'll have to go through adolescence all over again.'

At the door, there was the sound of someone clearing his throat.

'Sorry I'm late,' said the Doctor. 'Lost track of time.'

Mostly, there were hugs.

At one point, Amy did say: 'What took you so long?'

'Took me so long? Jane took me back more than five years, and broadcast an image of me several thousand years further back than that – I've had to wait around for all of you, passing time by defeating a few plots to destroy mankind but mostly waiting for all this to blow over,' said the Doctor. 'What took *you* so long?'

'Time travel,' said Rory. 'It's confusing, isn't it?'

And after they'd each told their stories, there was only one thing left to deal with. The Doctor had a leather holdall with him. He put it onto the desk that had once belonged to Jane Blythe and looked at the hopeful faces of Sameera and Nadia.

'I can't give you any extra time, Sameera,' said the Doctor sadly. 'When you paid it back to Jane, she took it all, and it's gone.'

'Oh,' said Sameera. She hadn't known until he said it that she'd been hoping so certainly – that she hadn't allowed herself to think otherwise – that this Doctor would be able to fix everything. And now, what, she was really 65 now?

The Doctor sighed. 'Those contracts really were watertight. They even managed to add on extra interest after you thought you'd paid it all back – interest accrued on the interest yet to accrue. According to this,' he produced a glass brick labelled Sameera Jenkins from his leather holdall, 'you still owe ten years.'

Sameera looked at the brick, with its faintly glowing motion at the centre. The Doctor placed another one next to it, labelled Nadia Montgomery.

'And as for you, Nadia,' he said, 'that broken watch of yours has done some very weird things to the contract. It seems to think you're owed another thirty years. Which would take you back to before you were born.'

Nadia stuck her lower lip out petulantly.

'So you can't do anything? I'll have to go through puberty again? And try to explain to my parents why I'm 10 years old now?'

The Doctor chewed his top lip. 'There is one thing,' he said.

He looked at the two bricks, side by side. Then he touched the tops of them and, very gently, lifted off their glass lids. He grinned.

'Turns out,' he said, 'only the owner can open them. Clever, eh?'

He reached inside both bricks and pulled out the contents.

They were flowing liquid glass spheres, each covered in some strange moving writing, each beating softly like a heart.

'Records of time. Time out of time, very hard to do. Wouldn't touch them if I were you,' he said as Amy reached out a finger towards one. 'Might get a nasty time-burn.'

He stared at the spheres, one in his right hand, the other in his left.

'This one says you owe ten years,' he nodded at Sameera's sphere on the right, 'and this one says you're owed thirty, so how about if we…' he crossed his hands over, 'presto chango! Where's a fez at a time like this?'

He dropped each sphere into the other brick very delicately, and popped the lids back on.

'Show me your watches,' he said, and Nadia and Sameera held out their hands. The Doctor took both their wrists, winked, and pressed the same button on each at the same moment.

There was a sort of sighing sound. Both of the beating

hearts of the glass blocks dissolved. And, without any fuss, Sameera was suddenly 35 again, and Nadia was 20.

'You'll have a bit of trouble explaining that,' the Doctor said to Nadia. 'A 40-year-old with the body of a 20-year-old. I suggest you say you went to a very exclusive clinic in Zurich.'

Nadia looked at her reflection in the office window. She grinned.

'I tell you what I think,' she said. 'I think the London office needs a new Head of Operations, someone who really knows the business. I think I'm the right woman for the job.'

'Just watch out for the credit crunch,' said Amy.

'The… what's that?' said Nadia.

'Oh, nothing,' said the Doctor, 'if anyone knows how to manage boom and bust, it'll be you.'

In the basement, Sameera and Andrew hugged the Doctor, Rory and Amy and watched them walk into the TARDIS.

'Is that really a spaceship?' said Andrew.

Sameera squeezed his hand. 'They're time-travelling aliens, why wouldn't their spaceship look like a police box?' she said.

'We're not all aliens!' protested Rory.

'No, Rory, only you are an alien,' said the Doctor, as the TARDIS door closed.

There was a *vworp, vworp, vworp* sound, and Sameera and Andrew were alone in Lexington Bank's sub-basement.

'What do you want to do now?' said Sameera.

Andrew shrugged.

'We could go for that promotion again, I suppose.'

Sameera looked at him, smiled and raised an eyebrow.

'What, endless competition against each other? Sounds great fun if we're all out of walls for us to bash our heads against.'

Andrew smiled. 'What do you really want, Sameera?' he said.

She took a deep breath, looked around her. 'I know it sounds stupid,' she said, 'but I've always really wanted to run a deli. One of those places where you can get anything. In a seaside town maybe. I know it'd be hard work but it'd also be real, do you know what I mean? Making something real, feeding people, sending them away happy. Something a bit useful in the world.'

Andrew nodded slowly.

'What about you?' she said.

'I always wanted to be a teacher,' he said at last, 'maybe teach music. Or science. I wanted to train after university but my results were good and my parents said I should talk to the careers adviser about my options and he told me to go for Lexington's and the money was so good that…'

'Yeah,' she said, 'I know. You got stuck. Just one more promotion, just one more round of bonuses. Me too.'

'So,' he said.

'So,' she said.

And he put his arm around her shoulders and kissed her lightly on the lips. And together they walked out of Lexington Bank for ever.

*

Like most thieves, the traders of the Time Market did have a sense of honour. Of a sort. They vowed solemnly to track down what had happened to the remainder of Jane Blythe in time and space. It was impossible that she'd vanished entirely – the traces of her existence proved that she had once existed, and if she'd once existed there was no reason to think she didn't still exist.

The Doctor had made them promise to find her. But, bureaucracy being what it is, the business proved arduous, time-consuming and ultimately fruitless. She was gone from the Time Market, they knew that. But any good Time Harvester will leave themselves just a little time in reserve. Just enough to start up in business again, somewhen else.

It was the sad conclusion of the Committee for Restoration of the Time Market, therefore, that it was impossible to track the harvester Jane Blythe. They found it unlikely, they said, that she would have been able to leave Earth. A close eye should be kept on the time streams of Earth for this reason, and they recommended the establishment of a Monitoring Team, whenever funds should be sufficient to do so.

They sent a copy of this report, as promised, to the Doctor's last known address – a storage facility under the Millennium Dome in London, Earth and, feeling that they had done all they could, went back to business.

In about 1985, just a year before the Big Bang changed the regulation of the London stock market and paved the way for the creation of previously unimaginable fortunes among the bankers of the City, the TARDIS materialised behind an abandoned warehouse on the Isle of Dogs, London. Elsewhere, the Doctor was in Foreman's Yard, 76 Totters Lane, dealing with some unfinished business. Once you can travel in time, being in two places at once is inevitable. And no business is ever finished.

The TARDIS door opened.

'So did we stop Lexington Bank collapsing?' Rory was asking.

'No,' said the Doctor. 'We just saved the Earth. The Bank will still crumble, but Nadia Montgomery will be able to rescue some of the business from the ashes. She's a smart woman.'

'And what about...'

'Just wait there for a moment,' the Doctor called back into the TARDIS. 'I'll only be a minute.' He stepped out.

The morning was bright and clear. The Doctor stuck his hands in his pockets and whistled a tune he'd learned a few centuries before as he sauntered towards a small door set into a warehouse wall. There was a piece of cardboard taped above a buzzer with a few words scribbled on it in black biro. The Doctor rang the bell and waited. Eventually, the door opened just a crack.

'Good to see you again,' said the Doctor.

'And you, Doctor,' said a smooth voice.

'Or do I mean, of course, good to meet you for the first time? Always get confused about those two.'

'It is all one. I let myself know you'd be coming,' said the voice.

'Did you let yourself know what I'd want too?' said the Doctor. 'I always seem to forget to give myself all the details, terrible habit, must try to keep a diary again.'

'You have an item you'd like me to secrete among another client's belongings?'

The Doctor pulled a slim pen-like package from his pocket and handed it into the darkness.

'I'll be delighted,' said the voice.

'Did we agree some sort of... payment?' said the Doctor.

'Oh Doctor,' laughed the voice. 'You do continue to amuse. Please, think nothing of it. I'm assured that at a certain point you will become a very valuable client indeed.'

'Right,' said the Doctor. 'That's... hmmm, that's... Right. Disturbing. Yes, best not to ask too many questions.'

From the darkness, there was a low and not entirely friendly chuckle before the warehouse door gently closed.

The Doctor started to walk back towards the TARDIS. He stopped, turned around, stared at the closed warehouse door. Took a pace or two toward it. Stopped. Stuck his hands in his pockets. Wrinkled his brow. Turned back and walked into the TARDIS.

Epilogue

Heemstede, The Netherlands, 1636

Marieke Jansen tore off her headscarf and ran her hands through her hair in frustration. She stared at the young boy who had brought her the news. It was too late in the season for this.

'What do you mean,' she said, 'no planters?'

The little boy wiped his dirty face with his dirtier hand.

'It's Mr Van Aerdenhout,' he said. 'He's hired all the men in the village for double wages.'

Van Aerdenhout. She should have known. He didn't need all those men; he'd probably hired them just to stop her getting her crop in the ground in the precious few perfect weeks.

Marieke and her husband had borrowed as many *guilder* as they could lay their hands on for the cargo of tulip bulbs. If they bloomed, if they produced offsets, this time next year they'd be able to sell the crop for fifty times what they'd paid for it. But only if the bulbs were planted in time. God in Heaven!

The boy was still waiting, winkling something unspeakable out of his nose with a grimy finger. She threw a *stuiver* to him, and he caught the coin handily, grinning as he left.

'I bet you wish there were ten of you!' he called back to her.

She did. She could get all those bulbs into the ground herself, if she had the time. It wasn't a hard job, just a long one, and needed to be done quickly.

There was a quiet cough from behind her.

She'd been sure no one was there, but when she turned round two men were standing on the porch of her farmhouse. They were well-dressed in long sober black coats with slashed sleeves letting the white shirt underneath show through, heeled black boots with bows on the front. They wore loose ruffs at their throats and neat pointed beards, every inch the gentlemen of finance.

'We hear you have a problem, Mrs Jansen,' said the first. 'You need more time.'

'Yes,' said the second. 'And my colleague Mr Hoogeveen and I hate to hear of a woman in need of more time when we can so easily assist.'

'Yes, my colleague Mr Verspronck and I have a little proposition for you, Mrs Jansen.'

'One we think you'll find it hard to refuse.'

'Hard even to think of refusing.'

'Hard,' said Mr Verspronck, 'even to imagine thinking of refusing.'

They laughed, in unison.

Mr Hoogeveen pulled a large pocket watch from his coat and held it out to Marieke.

'Now,' said Mr Hoogeveen, 'this is all very simple to understand…'

Acknowledgements

If this book is any good at all, it is mostly because of all the people who gave advice and interesting thoughts and read it very quickly and told me what was boring or incomprehensible. First of all thanks to Rebecca Levene, without whose input this would have been a book with almost no plot and precious little action. Pretty much everything that makes it readable is down to her. And enormous gratitude to my agent Veronique Baxter and to Justin Richards for expert guidance and shepherding through the process. And hundreds of thanks to Minkette, Dan Hon, Robin Ray, Adrian Hon, Yoz Grahame, Tilly Gregory, Phil Craggs, Julian Levy, Laura Hall, Marcus Gipps, Andrea Phillips, Una McCormack, Annette Mees, Leigh Caldwell and David Varela, all of whom supplied brilliant ideas, advice, support, and reassurance that my depiction of City life is entirely accurate. Apart from the aliens. Probably.

Thanks particularly to my mum Marion, who started everything one rainy weekend when she saw 'The Robots of Death' in Blockbuster and convinced me and my brother that an old episode of an old TV show was worth watching. After all, that's how it all started.

Author Biography

Naomi Alderman grew up in London and attended Oxford University and UEA. She is the author of four novels. Naomi's 2017 novel, *The Power*, was the winner of the 2017 Baileys women's prize for fiction. In 2006, she won the Orange Award for New Writers. In 2007, she was named *Sunday Times* Young Writer of the Year, and one of Waterstones' 25 Writers for the Future.

In 2012, she co-created the top-selling smartphone fitness game and audio adventure *Zombies, Run!* which is a market leader and has been downloaded millions of times. She is one of the presenters of *Science Stories*, a programme about the history of science on BBC Radio 4, as well as presenting many one-off documentaries.

Naomi is Professor of Creative Writing at Bath Spa University, has been mentored by Margaret Atwood as part of the Rolex Mentor and Protégé Arts Initiative, and in April 2013 she was named one of Granta's Best of Young British Novelists in their once-a-decade list. Her previous books have all been published by Penguin Random House.